Lost Girls
& Love Hotels

Lost Girls & Love Hotels

a novel

Catherine Hanrahan

HARPER ◉ PERENNIAL

NEW YORK • LONDON • TORONTO • SYDNEY

HARPER ● PERENNIAL

P.S.™ is a trademark of HarperCollins Publishers.

LOST GIRLS AND LOVE HOTELS. Copyright © 2006 by Catherine Hanrahan. All rights reserved. Printed in the United States of America. No part of this book may be used or reproduced in any manner whatsoever without written permission except in the case of brief quotations embodied in critical articles and reviews. For information address HarperCollins Publishers, 10 East 53rd Street, New York, NY 10022.

HarperCollins books may be purchased for educational, business, or sales promotional use. For information please write: Special Markets Department, HarperCollins Publishers, 10 East 53rd Street, New York, NY 10022.

FIRST EDITION

Designed by Paula Russell Szafranski

Library of Congress Cataloging-in-Publication Data
Hanrahan, Catherine.
  Lost girls and love hotels : a novel / Catherine Hanrahan.—
1st ed.
  p. cm.
  ISBN-10: 0-06-084684-4
  ISBN-13: 978-0-06-084684-8
1. Brothers and sisters—Fiction. 2. Schizophrenia—Fiction.
3. Tokyo (Japan)—Fiction. 4. Psychological fiction. I. Title.

PS3608.A7158L67 2007
813'.6—dc22   2005055108

06 07 08 09 10 ❖/RRD 10 9 8 7 6 5 4 3 2 1

For my parents
Mary and Robert Hanrahan

Lost Girls
& Love Hotels

PART ONE

The Outer Space Room

ometimes, when I'm staring down a room of Japanese stewardesses-in-training, looking across a sea of shiny black coifs, a chorus line of stockinged legs, knees together, toes to the side, when I'm chanting "Sir, you are endangering yourself and other passengers!," I think I should have let my brother stab me. I shouldn't have run when Frank came at me with the carving knife, yelling "Satan! Satan!" I should have faced him, arms outstretched, eyes closed in sacrifice, and let him put the blade into me.

I wake up to the sounds of Ines having sex in the next room. Ines is loud and she'll screw nearly anyone. If they don't meet her expectations, if she doesn't come three times, feel like she's transcended to a higher plane, speak in tongues, and get a postcoital foot rub, she makes them pay her. Cash. *"Fuck them, little shits. I deserve money if they waste my time!"* I used to be outraged. Used to think she was crazy. Now it all makes perfect sense. I sell my time and kill my body. She sells her body to kill time.

I look at the alarm clock. Ines has an orgasm. My bladder calls. It's time.

I have never, in my ninety-six days in Tokyo, been pressed into a subway car by the fabled white-gloved subway-pushers. I feel ripped off—it was just the sort of nightmare of modernity that I came to Japan to be a part of. That and drunk businessmen eating thousand-dollar sushi meals off the bodies of naked girls. Vending machines with school-girls' used panties on offer. Doomsday cults and death by overwork.

The morning train is all lolling heads and bad breath. It's cold season. Half the subway carriage wears surgeons' cotton masks. A forensics convention, hurtling through the tunnels.

Near Yoyogi station, I read a pornographic comic book over the shoulder of an old man. An octopus having its way with a girl in a kilt. A group of huge-eyed horny schoolboys is about to rescue her when the falsetto voice of the train conductor calls my station.

Air-Pro Stewardess Training Institute is on the fourth floor of the ABW Building. One floor above True Romantic Collection marriage agency and one floor below the offices of Toyama Waste Disposal. Two months ago, when I first started working at Air-Pro Stewardess Training Institute, still under the spell of Tokyo and jet lag, blissfully sleepless and anonymous, I liked the building. The strange ceramic-tiled exterior—like a giant inside-out bathroom. The tiny elevators that jerked and sputtered to their destination. I was happy to be somewhere where I couldn't understand a word, spared from the torture of random snippets of conversation. For a brief few days I used the word "lucky." Applied the word "lucky" to myself.

One day I asked one of the secretaries what ABW stood for. She smiled and gave me the address of the building, carefully wrote down the city, ward, and street number, as though I was an amusing idiot. "No," I said to her. "I know where it is, but what does it stand for." She smiled even more. "Yes. Standing," she answered. I've realized that ABW and most Japanese acronyms stand for nothing. They stand for the Roman letters themselves. Mysterious and sturdy and decorative. Sometimes, on my way to work, I invent my own meanings for ABW. Academy of Beauty and Weaponry. Abandon Belief Within. Acme Brain Wedgies.

I have realized that no matter what I do, Air-Pro Stewardess Training Institute will never fire me. So, I've been driven to dressing for shock value, like a petulant teenager—strolling into the lobby in ski pants and ballet slippers. The ski pants rustle when I walk. I like the way the

5

bib just barely conceals my little boobs and chafes my nipples a bit. I still have my platinum blond Louise Brooks–style bob that everyone thinks is so cute, but I've dyed the tips robin's-egg blue.

The staff scream "good morning" violently as the elevator doors open. I see them register my outfit. They struggle to maintain their professional smiles, but they shudder ever so slightly.

"Morning," I grunt, heading to the bathroom to change into my little blue suit.

Mikiko, the director's assistant, runs up behind me. Mikiko is fanatically cheerful, despite the tragedy. I heard about it from another staff member. She spoke about it in a hushed voice, the way some people talk about cancer or infertility. Mikiko is a failed flight attendant. With her degree from Tokyo University and her sylphlike figure, she made the cut for Japan Airlines—the dream of every Japanese girl with lofty ambitions. But during training, calamity struck. In the form of a cold sore. As the stress of her cabin-crew training grew, so did her blister. The doctors confirmed her worst fears. Herpes simplex 1. Her employers had no choice but to let her go. Pus-addled and dejected.

"Margaret-san! *O-genki desu ka?* You look so funky. Like a rock star, *ne?* You are really, really nitwit!" Mikiko says breathlessly.

"It's too early, Mikiko."

She follows me into the bathroom.

"Did you just call me a nitwit?"

"My boyfriend Kevin always says I'm nitwit. Like Meg Ryan. I love Meg Ryan. Do you love Meg Ryan?" Mikiko stares at me expectantly. She's a pretty girl with a bad over-bite. Since her double eyelid surgery, she has the look of a startled animal. I expect one day she will pounce on me, tear at my jugular. I keep my distance.

"Yes. Love her. I'm going to get naked now."

Mikiko just stands there, eyes popping, big white teeth tipped with hot-pink lipstick, resting on her lower lip. "I need some privacy," I whisper.

"Oh! Sorry! I have a good news. Today is starting a new recruit, Madoka-chan!" Here at Air-Pro, or trolley-dolly boot camp, as I refer to it, we call the students recruits. Our slogan hails, "Air-Pro. Putting young women in the air. Where they belong."

I struggle into my nylons and suit, scowl at my reflection in the mirror. I look like a slightly punk women's prison war-den. Matronly and freakish. Sitting down on the heated toi-let seat, I light a smoke and take out my mobile phone.

I've always believed that rituals are for fucked-up people with slippery grasps on reality. This is my latest ritual: each time I sit down on the toilet, I listen to the two saved mes-sages.

A dancing squirrel greets me when I turn on my phone. At first, I thought the squirrel was nauseatingly cute, but now, when I watch it pirouette across the tiny LCD screen, smiling maniacally, sly eyes and giant feet, I'm sure there's something malevolent about it. Ragging my neurosis with its electronic chirp. The phone has a function menu in English, but I prefer the Japanese. I've memorized the way each of the kanji ideograms look. The voice of the message-center computer, which sounds like someone trying to remain composed while being pinched very hard. The sequence of numbers I have to press to listen to the messages. To abort them midsentence. To save them. The whole process, after so many times, requires only a modicum of concentration. But I breathe deeply throughout, fix my attention on the patch of tile between my feet.

Message one. It's two months old. I've listened to it so many times I can recite the words in harmony.

Hello, Mags? This is Frank. I just wanted—your brother, Frank. I really wanted to thank you for the birthday card. Mags, can you call me? I have a new phone number. It's 1—that's the country code, 4-1-6— Mags, I got your card. It was so nice. Do you have my phone number? Okay, it's 4-1-6—5-4-5. Thanks for the card. Wait! You have to dial the country code. I have it here somewhere. This is Frank, Mags. Okay, so here's my number if you want to call. Did you know my birthday was last month? I'm a hundred and twelve years old. Margaret? Are you there?

I haul on my cigarette. Try to feel the rhythm of his mind, find some logic in his thoughts—speeding, merging, fracturing, forgotten. I'm sure there must be bliss in chaos. I'm banking on it. I wonder who sent him the birthday card. It wasn't me. I forgot.

Message number two. Mom. It's two weeks old, and I

haven't got all the way through it. I think that if I dissect the message, maybe I can disintegrate it. Return it back to tiny wavelets.

Margaret? Margaret I need you to call me. There's been an accident—

Stop.

Maybe if I keep it in parts, the whole will never touch me.

Save.

Ms. Nakamura, the school directors catches me in the hall-way.

"Margaret-san! *Aree!*" She eyes my hair. Nose scrunched up like I'm giving off a bad odor. "What happened to you? Never mind. We have a new recruit, Madoka-chan. This is a really big challenge for us. She is like a big chunk of stone."

"Stone?"

"You know what's inside stone?"

"I dunno. A diamond?"

"Flower! We will whip the flower out of her! Yes? Firm but kind. Let's go!"

Ms. Nakamura clickety-clicks down the hall. I'm sure Ms. Nakamura was born wearing heels. In her immaculate black suit, her skirt that constricts her stride to a practiced hobble, she looks like a tall woman who's been shrunk. Like a doll. Her hair is jet black and pulled up into a big mushroom, sprayed into taxidermic rigidity. One time I saw a strand of silvery-white hair that had escaped her attention. It snaked up from the nape of her neck and caught the light, glimmering like the inside of a seashell. I stared at it, mesmerized, until her creepy red talons were in my face, fingers snapping. "Margaret! Time to recite chicken or fish!"

Madoka is lingering outside the classroom, eyeing the advertisements—cosmetic dentists, photographers adept at creating shapely airbrushed ankles, hair-removal specialists, esthetics salons that use electrodes to zap fat. She's scratching the back of her calf with the heel of her shabby pumps.

"Madoka!" Ms. Nakamura calls. Madoka turns. "This is Margaret-sensei. She is a native English speaker!"

Madoka grabs my hand and shakes it too hard. My arm moves from the shoulder, like a rubbery string. Her smile is lopsided, pushed out on one side by a grayish snaggle-tooth. She's hiding a wad of chewing gum in the back of her mouth.

"Pleased to make you!" Her voice is jumpy like a child's, with a hoarse edge to it, like a little girl chain-smoker. "I'm so exciting," she says.

Ms. Nakamura's face quivers with a creepy little spasm. "Let's begin our training to become cabin crew," she pauses, giving Madoka an up-and-down look, "or worst-case scenario, ground staff."

I teach cabin-crew and airline-interview English, Monday to Friday. Teach is the wrong word. I *pronounce* cabin-crew and airline-interview English. Ms. Nakamura teaches the recruits what to say. She regards it as a science, arguing the primacy of the word "beverage" over "drink" with pointless dogmatism.

The classroom is filled with thirty girls, groomed within an inch of their lives, moving and speaking in precise, identical ways. Like a team of synchronized swimmers. Without water. I always feel a bit dirty around these girls. Their unlined skin and innocent minds. Shielded from birth by their families—shielded from the sordid world of drugs and unkempt foreigners.

Madoka makes her way to an empty chair in the front row, grinning madly, all teeth and gums, flopping into her chair with a loud sigh.

Ms. Nakamura clears her throat. "Recruits! Meet your new classmate, Madoka Wakiyama." The recruits chorus "Nice to meet you!" Madoka squirms in her seat. Her cheeks redden. Her eyes bulge. "Exciting," she mumbles.

Ms. Nakamura asks Madoka to tell the recruits about her hobbies.

"I like reading and tanning," she answers. Thirty manicured hands go to thirty glossy mouths, and a collective giggle fills the air.

"Don't you have a helping-people hobby?" Nakamura asks. Madoka tilts her head.

"Example! Rie! What is your hobby?"

Rie stands, lifts her chin. "I study sign language. I want to communicate with all people of the world."

Nakamura beams with pride. "And Sonomi?"

"My hobby is sign language. I want to communicate with all people of the world."

"Thank you, recruits." She addresses Madoka, "See? Helping people." She gives me a nod and I pick up my interview dialogue sheet.

"Listen and repeat," I drone. "I AM COMMITTED TO BECOMING A CUSTOMER SERVICE PROFESSIONAL." The recruits trill the words back, and I hear Madoka's voice above the others, loud and jerky. It sounds like an aria.

I'm six. Frank's eight. We're standing in front of a cage at a service station somewhere between Moncton and Halifax, looking at a monkey. We're on one of our marathon family road trips, driving from Toronto to Nova Scotia. Dad's afraid of flying. He claims most airline pilots are drunks and womanizers, that they're too busy nursing a hangover or goosing the stewardesses to be trusted with our lives.

Dad's about to pop a vein. The car's conked out again, and the mechanic tells Dad that he should sue the guy that sold it to him. "Ford Pinto," he says, shaking his head. "You'd be better off driving a sewing machine." My father works at a Ford dealership. He sold the car to himself.

Frank's standing a couple feet from the cage, hands at his hips, leaning forward and squinting. He wears Coke-bottle glasses that dwarf his head, glasses he's crushed or lost three times already.

"Actually, he's not a monkey," Frank says. "He's an ape. See? No tail. Monkeys have tails. Apes don't."

"Don't get too close," I say. Dad warned us: "You can look at the monkey, but DON'T GO NEAR THE CAGE!"

"He might be a gibbon," Frank says.

I take a long sniff of the air—the smell of gas and sweat and hands greasy with junk food. Looking over my shoulder, I see Dad, hands balled up, biceps flexed, stomach held in. Mom's lolling her head around, like she's working out the kinks in her neck, trying to look anywhere but at Dad.

"Look! He's thinking something," Frank says. The ape's head is tilted, shiny, black marbles of eyes scanning Frank's face. Frank takes a step toward the cage, and the ape points at him with its wrinkled black hand.

I hear Dad scream at the mechanic, "Just fix the goddamn car!" I turn to see Mom pulling at Dad's arm, Dad yanking it away from her. When I turn back, the ape has Frank's glasses.

I scream.

Dad jerks his head around. It takes a moment for him to register the scene in his mind. The ape is examining Frank's glasses, turning them in its strange, humanoid hands. It holds them up to its eyes and then pulls them away, grimacing.

"WHAT THE—!" Dad runs toward us and moves Frank out of the way. Frank wears a queer grin and touches the skin around his eyes.

14

"Okay," Dad says to the ape. "Come on now, give me the glasses." He's trying his best to sound soothing and calm, but he sounds kind of creepy and psycho. "Good monkey."

"He's an ape," Frank says.

"SHUT IT!"

The ape moves to the back of the cage and twists the wire frames. It holds one of the thick lenses between its teeth. Its lips curl back and it smiles. I think for a moment that Dad might cry, standing there impotently, his golf shirt soaked with sweat. After a minute or two, the ape hands the twisted frames to my father and spits out the lens with a loud "Puh-too!" Then it does what looks like a kind of dance around the cage. Dad holds the remains of the glasses at arm's length. The ape continues its dance, stops to scratch its crotch, and then, as if to add insult to injury, tilts its head back and lets out a high-pitched howl.

In the car, Dad keeps asking Frank questions without waiting for an answer. "Are you deaf as well as blind? I said 'DON'T GO NEAR THE CAGE!' What part didn't you understand? What kind of a moron are you anyway? Can you tell me that?"

Franks hangs his head. I wonder if he's crying. Dad keeps on for miles and miles. Every now and then, Mom interjects with "Come on, Ted," in a plaintive whine. Frank finally turns his face toward me, and I see he's smiling, contorting his face to conceal a laugh. He reaches over, grabs my hand, and squeezes.

I start out at Jiro's under the self-delusion that I'll have a few beers and go home. I start out with an image of myself in the morning, walking home from a tai chi class. Feeling like a cereal ad. Shoulders back. Chin up.

Jiro's has four stools and one wobbly table. It's on a busy corner near Roppongi station, but the entrance is hidden among a row of vending machines. Jiro's is the kind of place you could walk by a hundred times and not notice—those that do discover the place treat it like a secret hideout, a refuge. It's not much bigger than a bus shelter. But warmer. And stocked with booze. I'm a regular—the strange gaijin who drinks a lot. I sit in the last bar stool, next to the framed photograph of John Lennon. Jiro does his best to communicate with me with the English he's learned from Beatles' songs.

A trio of young construction workers occupies the bar

stools next to me. Tight spark plugs of bodies in bright knickerbocker pants. Leather split-toe construction slippers. A sprinkling of dust lies on them, like icing sugar. They sit lazily, pouring each other beer from tall bottles, raising their drinks to a lazy chorus of "*Kampai!*" Every few minutes, one of them steals a glance at me.

"Hard day's night, ne?" Jiro says, wiping the bar. A cockroach scuttles between my beer and me, and I flinch.

"Not dangerous," Jiro says, herding the roach around with a menu. "More clean than Koreans."

"Jiro!"

"I made a joke."

"That's not nice."

"*Gomen ne*! More clean than American."

"That's better."

I catch my reflection in the brass of the beer tap. And see what my face is doing. Contorting itself into a smile. Folding back into desperation like the snap of a rubber band.

I put a cigarette into my mouth, and Jiro has the match lit on cue. The smell of sulfur fills the tiny room. Jiro smiles. His face is like a parched riverbed—dry, deeply grooved, mud-colored. "Let it be," he says.

The alcohol hits me quickly, a familiar warmth spreading through my limbs, an uncoiling. I order another beer. The construction workers send over a cup of warm sake. Tonight I will get pissed, I decide.

I wonder how easy it would be to become a drunk, not a regular, functioning boozer, but a real one—a puffy-

17

faced, hollow-eyed hag, slurring insults at strangers, staggering wasted at ten in the morning.

"Where from?" one of the construction workers asks. He has sleepy, heavy-lidded eyes and an aerodynamic cowlick that lifts his hair off his forehead like a gust of wind.

"Narnia," I say.

"*So ka!*" He stares at me, his plump lower lip hanging down idly.

Jiro leans over the bar. "He loves you, yeah?"

"Yeah, yeah," I say, twirling my finger in the air.

"You have good eyes," Jiro tells me.

"You have good beer," I answer back. My voice is getting a slack booziness to it.

A roommate of mine told me once that she was sure I would eventually go mad. She was willing to bet on it. "You've got it in you," she said, emboldened by a six-pack of wine coolers. "Something about your eyes." She started laughing, the kind of laugh where no sound escapes except a low clicking from the throat. "My brother is schizophrenic," I said. She laughed harder. "He thinks the traffic lights are messages from outer space." She doubled over, moaning, eyes watering, waving her hand at me to stop being so funny. Funny. I figured, if I was destined to be crazy, at least it made good drunk conversation fodder.

The good part of drunk has passed. I'm struggling to focus my eyes. I think about the morning. The tai chi class seems unlikely. I imagine myself stumbling to the convenience store for a liter of Coke and a roll of antacid tabs. I wince at an olfactory premonition. The smell of me—pasty tongue, booze, smoke. Less like a cereal ad. More like a cautionary tale. -

The construction workers are slipping off their stools, barking things at one another, missing the glass when they pour beer.

Jiro's has a squat toilet. My motor skills are barely present. I lean my shoulder against the wall and slide down into a squat. Dial the phone with my nose. Try to direct the stream of pee away from my shoes. *There's been an accident . . . He got beat up Mags. You'd hardly recognize his face.*

Stop. Save.

I haven't recognized him for a long time.

In the narrow hallway leading from the toilets, I let the cowlicked one press me against the wall, his hand gropes around the buttons on my shirt, his mouth, open too wide, like he's trying to get a good bite of a big apple, teeth hitting teeth with a disturbing scrape that's loud inside my head. The feeling of being touched, the sound of his voice, mumbling through the kiss "*Suki, suki*" (I like, I like)—the awkwardness of it all makes me want to cry.

I think about taking him home. I imagine his body under the poofy construction pants and jacket. Something hard to weigh me down. But it's too early. Barely ten. I have to let the night drag me on. I put my hand to his chest and push him away, surprised by the willingness with which he retreats. Surprised, too, by the draft that rushes down the narrow passageway and cools my skin. I indulge myself for a moment, then walk away to pay the tab. It's time to find Ines and switch intoxicants.

I'm six. Frank's eight. In the basement, in the strange light of the makeshift tent. Lawn chairs and old sheets. Silverfish and mold. Frank with his thumb in his mouth, safe with the knowledge that Dad won't come down here and call him a baby. He'll stand at the top of the stairs and bellow if we're needed for din-din. I honestly wonder if Frank's full name is "For Christ Sake Frank." No one ever says my name. I could be invisible. I like the idea.

Frank lies on his stomach, up on his elbows, *Guinness Book of World Records* open in front of him. Slurs the words around his pruney thumb. "Sidar Chillal of India holds the world records for longest fingernails. Measuring 20 feet 2.25 inches."

"He'd give good back scratches," I say.

"Uh-uh. Look." In the upside-down photo, Mr.

Chillal's brown wrinkly hands sit on a table, yellow fingernails coiled like corkscrews next to a ruler.

I squeeze my eyes shut. Worry that Mr. Chillal will show up in my nightmares. "Ewww," I say.

"Cool huh?" Frank says.

The thump of footsteps upstairs. Shouting. Words I can't make out. I think this is how adults talk. In shrieks and expletives. Tears and slammed doors. That all conversations end in one person going for a drive, or two people retiring for an impromptu nap. Squeaking beds and extra showers.

"Let's have a fight," Frank says.

"But you're bigger than me."

"Not a fistfight." He sits up cross-legged. Takes his thumb from his mouth. "Like this." He closes his eyes and takes a deep breath. Opens them and screams, "How can you be so goddamned stupid?"

My back straightens. "I'm not stupid."

Frank smiles. "Good. Good," he whispers. His face gets hard again. "If I have to pay another bill from your harebrained shopping trips so help me God."

"But—"

"But, but," he mocks. "I work all week. What do you do?"

"—"

"Tell me. What do you do besides get fatter?"

I stand up and the tent starts to come down. I can't get out.

"Useless!" Frank says.

21

Tears rush to my eyes, and Frank pulls me down by my wrist. Goes through the motions of kissing me. His mouth clamped shut, rubbing his face on mine. My heart is beating too fast. I've never noticed it in my chest before.

Frank stands up and adjusts the sheets around the lawn chairs. "That's completely gross," he says, wiping his mouth on his sleeve. "I don't know how they can do that."

Sounds have died upstairs. I still try and listen. Creaky bedsprings and quiet reproaches.

Frank holds his finger in the air. "Ding! Ding! Ding!" He holds the book close to his face. "Quiz time!" Presses the book to his chest and adjusts his eyeglasses on his nose. "The smallest woman in the world was how tall?"

I think about small. So small I could hide in the cracks in sidewalks, in the space between the bed board and the mattress. So small my ears couldn't pick up sound.

"Hint," Frank says. "Smaller than you." His glasses slip down on his nose again.

Smaller than me. Frank looks anxious. I think of numbers. Something bumps upstairs. I look at my blobby arms. Think of dolls. The quiet of dollhouses. The basement door opens, and I wait for the scream.

t doesn't take long to find Ines. Like we are connected by a homing signal. Except it never leads us home.

"Sweetheart," Ines says. Ines, no matter how drunk she gets, no matter what kind of dive she's drinking in, always looks like a cosmetics advertisement. As though someone is following her around with a soft pink light. She's wearing tight jeans tucked into a pair of black biker's boots. A sheer pink blouse open to below the level of her bra, her black hair falling in ropy tendrils over her shoulders. She's the kind of girl who never inspires envy so much as awe. The way one looks at a lean, smooth panther roaming the Serengeti in *National Geographic*. She is another species altogether. "I danced for some gangsters tonight and got a tippy-tip," she says. Opens her purse. Ciggies. Lipstick. Five condoms. And a Ziploc of white stuff. Cocaine is a rare commodity in Japan. But Ines always seems to have some.

We head to the washroom. As we pass the bar, a tall black man hands me a plastic flower. "I'm not in love," he tells me. "I *am* love." I want to tell him to keep it to himself, but Ines has my hand. Dragging me across the dance floor. The air changes in the thick of the bodies. I glance now and then at the faces. Blissful swaying heads. Shut eyes. Misery clothed in ecstasy.

In the toilet stall, hope arranges itself in little lines. I can almost feel the dopamine engage. Like a Pacman gobbling up my angst. It'll take a lot of gobbling to make a dent. I glance at Ines's watch. Eleven-ten. Still so early. Time flies when you're having fun. Time seems to crawl for me always.

I crouch and examine myself in the shiny silver of the toilet-paper dispenser.

"How much farther to rock bottom?" I ask Ines.

"You think too much," she says, handing me a tube of lipstick. "Pretty yourself up."

You wander around the bar for a while. The music is good and it's just getting better. A queer mix of techno and Japanese pop—bleeps, blips, and strange words. You find a place to stand. To call your own. A boy reaches out as he walks by and he touches your hair. "Like a baby hair," he says, and you smile. The smile erupts from somewhere around your belly. And a light goes on. Miraculously, it's that time of the night—shortly after one—when life seems full of possibility. You don't know how or why you ever felt low, ever felt hopeless, ever felt anything less than a goddess, sculpted from ivory, imbued with a cutting wit and a sensitive soul. You reek of sex appeal. Everyone is here to see *you*. You've been sent to Japan, you surmise, to show them exactly what hot is.

You drift away from the post you were leaning against. You don't need anything to hold you up. Oh, the buoyancy of the night! As you move through the crowd, all eyes are on you. Anybody here could be yours for the evening, but you don't need sex—you are beyond sex, you are, in fact, beyond physicality—although you are astonished at how good your body looks.

You're talking to a guy from Minnesota, who teaches at a university you've never heard of.

"My main area of interest is contrastive linguistics," he tells you. "I mean, determining why culture undermines language acquisition. Why people fail to communicate."

The words seem to dance out of his mouth. Trying to concentrate makes you dizzy. A little nauseous.

He twitches. "Am I boring you?"

"No, no." For a moment, you get lost in a pocket of time. Stare off toward the shooter bar and wish you could go back six drinks and four snorts of coke. Back to the effervescence and hope of the two-beer buzz. "Can you buy me another champs, darling?" you say. More booze to hold back the self-loathing.

Ines holds court with a huddle of Greek or Brazilian or Israeli boys. Fuck, she's gorgeous. When you go over, she kisses you on both cheeks and then square on the lips. The boys squirm. Ines is so French. The name, the accent, the long legs and effortless style. She's from Calgary, but what does geography matter?

"I'd like to introduce you to Giorgio," she says, waving her hand in front of her man-harem.

"Which one's Giorgio?"

She gives you a quizzical look. Bunny wrinkles on her nose. "Oh they all are."

Ines is *so* funny.

Then you ask the question. "I need another toot. Where's the stuff?"

Ines laughs. "It's gone, lovey. That's it. Gone. Bye-bye."

In an instant, you are you again.

I start to power-drink. Sake in one paw, beer in the other. Try to backpedal to wasted. Neurotransmitters starving for white food. Like a zombie I wander onto the dance floor. I don't understand why everyone in Japanese clubs dances facing the DJ, as if it was live music, as if there was something to see. Then it hits me—no one here is on drugs. They are all here for the music. *For the music!*

Then again, I am here for the music, too—because the music matches the drugs I'm on. Was on. In fact, the music matches me—the thumping bass-beat, the spiraling rhythm. It seems to be building toward something, up and up, toward some release, some moment of catharsis. But it just spirals, back eventually to where it started. I'm not building toward anything at all.

The crowd is thinning. My eyes are drawn to the sad collection of debris on the dance floor. Some straws and discarded cocktail napkins. Abandoned event flyers. The room seems too big. Too bare.

In the bathroom, the line of girls chirrup at their reflection. Little speakers in the stalls broadcast flushing noises to disguise the tinkle of pee. Taped to the hand dryer is a missing-girl flyer. I've seen it before. A blonde with shiny lips and tweezed eyebrows. A dead girl, most likely. I drop my head. Study the floor tiles. I can feel the dead girl's stare. *Stop it*, I think. *I'm trying to have a good time.*

When I finally get a stall, I yank at my tights and sit down. Someone sprays perfume, and the scent wafts over— a sweet, juvenile smell—vanilla and fruit salad. I stab at my mobile phone. Fold over and lean into the earpiece. Listen to Frank. Some American girls rush in, all sweat and twang. One of them says, "You know the definition of insanity is doing the same thing again and again and expecting different results." The tap comes on. *I'm a hundred and twelve years old.*

"Then we're all fucking nuts," the American girl replies.

I know what you mean, I think. Me, too.

You'd hardly recognize his face. Happened at some sports bar on The Danforth. He'd stopped taking his drugs and—

Enough. Save.

Flush.

I know my rule: When coming down from drugs, do not

gaze upon oneself in a mirror. I always ignore my rule. But I'm used to what I see. Baggy eyes and sallow skin. A sinful waste of youth. I fashion my fingers into a rake and tend to my hair—pull the fringe down heavy over my forehead. If I squint and hold my head at a certain angle, I manage to look sexy. A blue Pat Benatar. If I stand back and think, *I loathe you all*, I look even better. A shrunken runway model after a three-day drug binge.

A Japanese girl asks me if I can use chopsticks. Then she asks if she can please squeeze my boobs, holding her cupped hands out to me. "Sure," I say. Pull my shoulders back a little. The girl gives me a little grope, scuttles like a crab back to her friends, and I realize that I am no longer above physicality. I need sex.

You bring Masa (or Hiro, or Toshi, or Takuya) home. He was the best of the desperados lingering around the bar after the ugly lights had been turned on. Try to explain in beginner's English that you want to be tied up and gagged. You hold out a necktie and a bandanna to him. He looks at you like a baby bird fallen from the nest. Gestures—hands above your head, wrists together, approximation of arousal on your face. His pupils dilate. He blushes. The idea seems to snap into place in his mind and, like most of them, he's all over it, all over you, and finally you're getting wet.

You like it like this because the guy, the body on top of you with a penis and a pulse, won't pretend to be tender, won't pretend he loves you, or even likes you. He won't pretend anything at all, because you've given him permission not to. Yeah sure, if he's angry, if he hates his mother, hates his job, his life, the world, you might end up with bruises. If he's smart, the bruises won't show when you're dressed. But mostly, you like it like this because it's the only thing that turns you on.

He has lost all gross motor control, he's all over the place, one knee on the futon, one knee on the floor, fumbling with the necktie that still has a knot in it from last time and looks like a noose. He yanks at the knot with his teeth, apologizes in polite Japanese, jerks his head to the side, sighs in exasperation. You're not sure whether this is fun or tragic. "Give it to me," you mumble through the gag. Lucky you started smoking again and stopped biting your fingernails. Yank. Twist. The tie is unknotted. "Now fuck me please."

The guy sits down at the edge of the futon, his chin drops.

You pull the bandanna from your mouth. "What is it?"

"*Gomen*—. I can't."

You wriggle out of your constraints, sit up, and light a smoke.

"I want to know your mind," he says.

"No you don't."

"*Maji-de*. It's true. I'm interesting."

"Bet you are. Now go home."

"No."

"Run along, now," you wave at him. "Shoo!"

He gives you a look. Something between need and pity. For a moment, you think about asking him to spoon you. Your body assumes the position. He looks down at you like a parent at a sick child. You close your eyes, imagine being laid out on a slab, pink and vulnerable. The door clicks shut and you are safe. Alone.

The alarm clock casts a strangely comforting green glow over the tiny room. 5:29. Nothing good ever happens between five and six. You feel the hangover lying in wait, the drugs exiting your body like bugs under your skin. If you were smart, you'd prepare for the morning, soften its punch with a glass of water and an ibuprofen by the bedside. You'd wash off your makeup, so you wouldn't look like Alice Cooper when you wake up.

But you're not smart.

You plop your thumb in your mouth and instantly connect to something else, throw a switch in your psyche and you are back, way back, before all the bad choices, the wrong turns. Nestle the pad of your thumb against the nubby landscape of your palate, hook your index finger over your nose, leave the rubble of the present, and retreat to an imagined past.

I'm eight. Frank's ten. Dad has a new job selling luxury vehicles. New job, new house. A monster home with a spiral staircase, a Jacuzzi, and a garage big enough for another family. Frank closes his eyes when we drive through the subdivision—there are no streets, only drives and points, circles, cul-de-sacs—"Makes me dizzy," he says. All the houses. All the same.

Our front lawn is still unsodded, the faux Victorian cornices unpainted. Something about the contractor. Mom and Dad fight about it all the time.

Christmas is coming, and today is family-photo day. In a month or so, the fireplace mantle will be chock-a-block with family photo cards. Perfect families lounging by crackling fires, wearing argyle sweaters and bibbed velvet dresses. Shiny-haired, straight toothed, button-nosed families. We have to make our card. Dad is stressed. Frank and I get uglier every year.

Sometimes, when we're all sitting around the kitchen table—Frank with his bug eyes and skin condition-du-jour, twitching and jabbering until Dad says "Quit it," me like an overgrown baby, bloated and fleshy—Dad looks us over and seems to deflate. Unsuck his stomach. Take off his smile like a too-tight uniform. Things have not turned out as he'd planned. We have not turned out.

Mom's still pretty. Big eyes, big boobs, big auburn hair that looks silky but feels crispy. On a good day, she looks like a tired twenty-five-year-old. Most days, she looks like someone standing in the middle of an intersection, the light turning yellow, the bottom of her brown-paper grocery bags fallen out, cans rolling into traffic, a carton of eggs smashed at her toes. A person whose day has fallen to pieces. Every day.

They make a nice couple, Mom and Dad. If they rented a couple of Sears catalogue kids, if Mom took one of her pills and Dad had a three-finger scotch, they'd make a nice photo.

Mom's rubbing Frank's scabby chin with a vinegar-soaked rag, trying to get the crust off so she can put the ointment on so the impetigo doesn't take over his face. Frank doesn't move. Doesn't cry or flinch or anything. The doctor says his face is contagious. He's been excused from school. Frank hates staying home. I think he's lucky—school is a nightmare of extroverts and dodgeball.

Dad comes downstairs in his chinos and forest-green

shirt, red-and-green-striped rep tie, Sperry Topsiders. Barrel-chest. Burt Reynolds mustache. He takes one look at Frank sitting motionless on the stool, Mom with her yellow dish-gloves and blood-soaked rag. "Oh for Christ's sake, Liz. Today?"

"Ted—"

"How's that going to look in the photo? Open sore! Happy holidays!"

"I have to remove the crust or—"

Dad holds up his palm. "Okay. Okay. I'm going to eat now."

It's my turn now.

"Margaret, why aren't you dressed?" Dad whines.

Mom sighs. "Get dressed Mags."

I start thinking about the hypnosis record. Frank plays it sometimes on the old record player. He says you don't need a pocket watch at all, just a soothing voice and a firm stare. I think about the sound of the record. The Indian man's voice. *Fizz-clop. Fizz-clop. Your body is heavy, heavy. Sink into it. Fizz-clop.* Dad pours some cereal into a bowl, but it comes out too fast, overflows onto the counter, the floor.

I can't move.

Mom frowns. "Mags! Go! Giddy-up!"

Feel the pull of gravity.

Dad slams the cereal box down. "What's wrong with you?"

I look at Frank, at his blank stare, at his raw chin, at Dad's cereal, Mom's gloves. The smell of vinegar and blood and peanut butter fills my nose. Saliva floods my mouth and I think, *No please no please no.* Frank turns his head and looks at me. Smiles. *It's okay.* Hands on my knees, face down. I throw up my Captain Crunch on the faux Spanish tiles. It splatters and hits the knees of Frank's dress pants, the hem of Mom's Christmas dress. Frank doesn't move. Mom pulls her gloves off. Dad says "Damn!" I feel the pull of gravity.

Down.

Down.

wake up to the drone of the little man crawling through the neighborhood in his truck at twenty kilometers an hour, moaning into his loudspeaker, "*Yaki-ii-MO, Yaki-ii-MO!*" The song is so depressing. The first time I heard it, I thought it must be a Japanese death cult recruiting members. It was saddening to find out the banal truth—he was only hawking tubers. The song, the "Sweet potato, delicious sweet potato!," is getting louder.

I'm still in the numb phase of my hangover. Brain scooped out. Belly screaming for food.

I throw my robe on. *Where's the sash?* Shit. Some guy left me in bed one night with the sash tied around my ankles—so tight my feet swelled up. Ines had to rescue me, cut the sash off me with a pair of nail scissors. It was a running joke for two weeks.

The truck is almost at the corner when I reach the street,

the low sad song trailing away. I scream after it. "Hey! Wait! *Chotto matte!* Hello. *Moshi moshi!*" I laugh at my word salad of Japanese and English. My slippers go *flop! flop!* as I run, one hand in the air, waving madly, the other clutching my robe so I don't flash the neighborhood.

The truck stops, and I walk panting toward the little man, whose face is frozen in an expression revealing horror, delight, and confusion.

"*Futatsu o kudasai,*" I say, holding up two fingers. The smell of the roasted sweet potatoes fills my nose. Smoke billows up from the back of the truck.

The withered little troll sings thank-you, hands me the paper bag with both hands, steals a peek at my bare legs when he bows.

A sudden and bizarre urge overtakes me—to skip back to the house, click my heels like Frank and I used to do as kids. It was fine for me to do it, to yelp and click, but Dad said Frank looked like a little faggot. Eventually we stopped clicking altogether. Walked like normal people. I resist the urge.

When I get inside, I realize I'm turning Japanese. I look down at my feet, at my "Cherry Girl" room shoes—the kind with little plastic reflexology nubs on the insoles, the kind emblazoned with a cheerful half-mouse, half-human, apple-cheeked cartoon character—I look down and feel a little wave of horror. I've worn my room shoes outside! I've contaminated my "Cherry Girl" room shoes with outside dirt. I've already stepped up from the *renkan*, the all-important two-foot-square space that separates the *outside* from the *inside*. The outside dirt and chaos is on my "Cherry Girl" room shoes. I'm bringing it inside. Not sure what to do, not sure why I even care, I take off my "Cherry Girl" room shoes and carry them upstairs.

The-Guy-Whose-Name-Nobody-Knows is shuttling yet another Japanese girl out of his room. To her horror, we meet at the top of the narrow staircase. The-Guy-Whose-Name-Nobody-Knows shuttles girls out of his room several times a week. Different girls. Usually late at night or early in the morning. They do the walk of shame down the length of the yellow-walled hallway, past the sour-smelling row of toilet rooms, down the stairs to the front door. Sometimes I listen for the passionless little kiss before the door closes, for the awkward exchange of mobile phone numbers. After they leave, The-Guy-Whose-Name-Nobody-Knows usually goes into the kitchen and nukes a frozen burrito. He tells me twice a week how to order frozen burritos and canned ravioli from the Internet. They are, he insists, "a lot cheaper than that Japanese shit."

The guy says little else to me or anyone else in the house. We are simply ugly reminders that he is not the exotic, globe-trotting, boy-band-member look-alike that he likes to think he is. He is doughy and pale. During the week, he wears bad suits that don't fit properly, and on the weekend, bad jeans that don't fit properly. He has many T-shirts that advertise the many exotic places he's visited. On nights he isn't fucking Japanese girls, he probably reads his passport, wishes the high school jocks could see him now. One long-haul flight and he's gone from zero to hero.

The girl being shuttled has buck-teeth that distort her otherwise doll-like face. She walks like a wind-up toy. Squeaks a little when we meet on the stairs. Her hand assumes the mouth-shield position—Japan's answer to orthodontics. I smile at her. She bows at me. The-Guy-Whose-Name-Nobody-Knows puts his hand on the small of her back, urging her forward, urging her out. The sweet potatoes smell sweet. "*Kirei desu*," I say to the girl being shuttled. You're pretty.

I don't want to listen for the passionless kiss or the mobile phone tango. I want to eat my sweet potatoes and enjoy my strange blend of melancholy and contentment. I know it won't last. It's a fine balance, struck when the precise amount of intoxicant produces a temporary amnesia, a dulling of the capacity to fixate, deconstruct, analyze. When life is reduced to this step, then that step, to the way water tastes to a dry mouth, the way kindness comes easily at these times, fits into the moment like a lover's body curling into mine. When life is not out there. It's here. And here. And here.

I want to enjoy it while it lasts, before the midday plummet, when my only recourse will be to sleep or buy useless shit.

I try to ignore the dinginess of the hallway, the yellowing stippled walls, the hemorrhaging garbage bin under the PUT YOUR CLAP HERE sign. I try to laugh at the fact that I live in a flophouse by Japanese standards. By any standard. I tell myself that everything is experience, that someday I'll see all of this as part of a puzzle, that it will amount to something, that *I* will amount to something. For a moment, my mind starts up that old neural pathway, toward despair, toward worst-case-scenario territory, but I make it to Ines's door in time.

The door is ajar, so I burst in and hold the bag of potatoes over my head like a trophy. I'm afraid I'm manic, but I push the thought aside, swim awhile in my sudden energy, the excitement only aromatic vegetables can engender. "Ta-da!" I scream, attempting a click, failing, almost toppling over. My robe falls open and I stand there all goose bumps and hard nipples, panting, close to happy for the first time in months. I'm not sure why. I don't care.

"Good morning gorgeous," Ines says with a purr. She looks perfect. Makeup unsmudged, not a hair astray. "This is Kazu." Ines pulls back the duvet and reveals a brown smooth man, painted with tattoos, ropy with muscles, curled in the fetal position, sound asleep.

"Oh shit, sorry."

"Don't be silly. *Entrée*. What've you got there?"

"*Yaki-iimo,*" I whisper. Steam puffs out of the bag when I open it. "Who's the guy?"

Ines grabs my hand, giggles, nibbles at the sweet potato. "Kazu. I think he's a gangster or something. Very dangerous."

I look at Kazu, his shaved head, pouty lips, high, broad cheekbones. Something about him triggers an uncomfortable animalism in me, erases for a moment all my accumulated angst, and transforms me into a walking appetite. I let my breath go. Try to collect myself. Tell myself he'll wake

up and say something unsexy in pigeon English and all will
be as it should be.

"Mmmm," Ines says. She flashes me her cum face—chin
up, mouth open, eyelids fluttering. "Fuck this is good."

"I bet."

"No this." She takes another bite, runs her hand over
Kazu's shoulder. "*And* this." His eyes open.

The sweet potato tastes like candy.

"*Ohayo gozaimasu,*" Kazu says.

"Good morning baby." Ines kisses his smooth head. My
chest feels hot. "This is my friend. Isn't she yummy?"

I pull my robe tight across my body.

"Threesome? What do you think, sweetheart?"

I breathe in a noseful of the air— Chanel No. 5 and cor-
poreal indulgence. Hope that Ines will dismiss her sugges-
tion with a laugh. The sober light of the morning is not the
time for a threesome.

Kazu stretches like a cat. The cords of his neck tighten.
"Time is?"

"Ten," I spit out. So pleased to respond to him.

He sits up. Cracks his neck. Left. Right. I wonder if he
really is a gangster. Ines is prone to exaggeration, and there
is something sophisticated about Kazu. Something in his
movements—the delicacy with which he lifts his body from
the bed—that doesn't seem fit for a gangster.

"I must go," he says.

Ines pouts. "So soon?"

I catch myself slack-jawed. Saliva collecting in the
trough of my lower lip. Embarrassment crawls on me like

ants. "I'll go— give you some space," I say. In the mirror propped up at the end of the bed, I catch my reflection. Mascara smeared under my eyes, blotchy skin, crazy medusa hair. *Fuck.* I scamper across the tatami mats, close the door behind me, lean on it, and suck air into my lungs. For a second, my eyes go squirrelly and the walls seem to pulse and buckle with my breathing.

Kazu.

I'm nine. Frank's eleven. It's a year before Dad leaves. All the signs are there. Mom and Dad are like animals in a too-small cage. Frank and I are the runts of the litter. Trampled in their battles.

"Shake my hand," Dad says suddenly at dinner. He stretches his hand across the table to Frank. Dad's on a mission to make Frank a man. I'm not sure what an eleven-year-old man would be like, but apparently sports are important. And standing up straight. "Losers slouch" is the word around the house.

"Oh for God's sake, Ted," Mom says. "Can we eat in peace, please?"

"Shake it Frankie." Dad jerks his arm.

Frank half rises, sticks his spindly arm out. He's grown. Taller, not bigger. His fingers are long and bony. The underside of his elbow is red with eczema.

43

"Mom, why don't we have music playing at dinner? Like at restaurants," I ask.

Frank slips his bluish hand into Dad's hairy red one.

Mom smiles. "That's a good idea Mags." She stands up quickly and scampers into the kitchen on her tippy-toes. It's her "I'm-angry-and-exhausted-and-undervalued-but-I'm-going-to-be-cheerful-goddamn-it" walk.

Frank takes a few shallow breaths and gives Dad a limp handshake. Dad looks expectant, like there's more to come. There isn't more.

The Captain and Tennille play on the radio in the kitchen.

"If you want to get anywhere in this world," Dad says, "you have to have a firm handshake. Rule number one. It's simple."

Mom sits back down, arranges her cloth napkin on her lap, straightens her back. "More ham anyone?" The beast sits in the middle of the table, adorned with pineapple slices and cloves.

Dad's hand goes out again. "Here, Frank, watch me."

"Mom, I can't stop imagining the pig's head and tail," I say.

Dad shakes Frank's hand firmly. A grin sprouts on his red face and collapses again into his normal glower. "See?"

"That kind of hurt," Frank whines.

Tennille sings "Do That to Me One More Time."

"Now you try Frankie." Dad's arm is twitchy with sinew and vein. Once is never enough.

Frank takes a deep breath, puts his hand in Dad's, and

squeezes, suddenly and violently. I can see Frank's fingers strain. Dad's hand compresses, his fingers fold into one another, his Adam's apple bobs. I can almost hear a crunch.

"Good job, son," he says.

Frank smiles.

Dad is redder than usual. "Okay, that's good."

"Can we eat by candlelight?" I suggest. "Like in *Hart to Hart*?"

Mom sighs. "Let go Frank."

For a second I can see the white imprint of Frank's hand on Dad's when he releases his grip.

"Better," Dad says, giving his hand a stretch. "Better."

"Candlelight?" I say again.

Mom poises the knife over the beast. "Maybe next Sunday, hon."

The dead girl has put me on edge. Suddenly she's everywhere. And nowhere. She vanished a month ago, and her picture has started to pop up all over Tokyo. She peeks out from collages of rave flyers, posters for art exhibitions, J-pop singles, suicide hotlines. In the trains, she looks down from the gossip magazine adverts, a disembodied head eyeing the groggy human cargo. It's always the same photo, a head-and-shoulders shot, her eyes dead-center, following me wherever I stand. Her mouth is curled up at the corners into a Mona Lisa grin, as if she's hoarding a secret. Only she knows where she is. Running. Hiding. Captive. Dead.

Sometimes when I go clubbing, high on something, with the dead girl staring down at me from giant electronic billboards, I silently curse her. She's a downer, grinning beside her vital statistics, warning me, taunting me.

Whenever my eyes meet hers, I feel like I'm turning to liquid, seeping into the cracks and crevices of the world—
afraid I'll never be able to retrieve my damp remains when
I choose to get a life.

So I troll the city. A different neighborhood every
Sunday. On Sundays, I love Tokyo. It opens like a flower
for me, parades its multiplicity before me—cute Japanese
boys with artfully streaked and teased hair; designer bag–
carrying office ladies walking pigeon-toed in kitten-heeled
mules; *kogaru*, the deeply tanned bad girls, frosty-lipped
and glittering; kimono-clad old ladies, plucking their
mobile phones from bamboo-handled handbags. On
Sundays, the broad boulevard of Omotosando is like Paris.
Paris with its history erased and rewritten by a schizophrenic comic-book artist.

I always start out in Ikebukuro, at the Sunshine
Building. The elevator to the sixtieth floor goes dark when
the doors close, phosphorescent stars appear on the walls,
on the ceiling. I feel like I'm floating, like the carriage will
take me somewhere other than a room with lots of windows and an overpriced canteen. The white-gloved elevator
girl chirps something inconsequential, something vaguely
sensual in her little-girl singsong. The ride never lasts long
enough.

From the windows, I get a three-sixty of the city. Tokyo
from above looks like the insides of a machine, mammoth
and gray. No square of space goes unused—buildings seem
compressed, squished together like commuters on a rush-
hour train. The traffic, even on a Sunday, coils through the

city in one long centipede. Small patches of green look wrong. They should be removed—like photos of an old lover—they only cause bouts of melancholy, craving, attachment.

For my ten-dollar admission fee, I get a handy reference map, a photo of the tangled machinery of Tokyo with cute cartoon koala bears marking points of interest. I look out at the city that stretches out farther than I can see, stretches out into an eerie moonscape, the dirty floss of pollution obscuring still more of it. I imagine that it's a maze, that there's a way in, a way out, that the dead girl is trapped somewhere in a nightmare of dead ends. I look down at the map and choose a place to get lost in.

Sometimes I end up in Shimokitazawa. Wander the narrow little streets around the station. Go from secondhand clothing shop to café to secondhand clothing shop. The Japanese in Shimokitazawa are a bit looser than the rest of the Tokyoites. The men in straw hats and Hawaiian shirts. Girls in dreadlocks and clothes from India. Smelling of incense and escape. I stay until I'm wired on coffee and the jazz clubs open up. Blow half a week's wages on the table charge and ten-buck beers. Sway a little to the whine of the saxophone.

Other days, it's out into the suburbs, to the rent-a-dog park, where I pay thirty bucks to lead around a confused-looked beagle for two hours. Watch housewives freak out when their rent-a-dog assumes the pooping posture. They lay out a neat square of paper towels on the grass and then wipe the poor beast's bum with wet-naps. The whole surreal spectacle of it inevitably leads me to the nearest bar. After a few glasses, I start to concoct drunken schemes to liberate the rent-a-dogs. Balaclava and ninja slippers. Wire clippers and Milk Bones. Dogs following me around the city, like a weak-livered Moses.

Today I'm in Jimbocho, the book district. The shops overflow with words—there are comic-book stores, cookbook stores, shops with musty ancient tomes, others with hardcore porn proudly displayed, unabashedly browsed. The pedestrians in Jimbocho seem uniformly beige as they wind through the narrow streets, pausing at the little tables set up outside the storefronts, looking for stories, waiting to be colored in like paint-by-numbers.

I find a shop that sells English books, ride the phone booth–sized elevator up six floors, and lose myself in the stacks. And there is Kazu. Crouched down in the classics section, his head turned at an awkward angle, reading the spines. His shoes are shiny. His feet small. Through the neatly pressed white linen of his shirt, I can see the faint purple outline of his tattoos, the bulge and twitch of the muscle that runs down his side. Something about his body, the brutal bulk of his neck, his legs, emanates violence. But his movements, the way he runs his hands over the books— slowly, as though he might wake them—is delicate, almost girlish.

He's in my territory, surrounded by English. I feel emboldened, and walk over to him, stand so close that his knee nearly brushes my shin.

"Remember me?" I ask, conjuring up the words from my throat. They come out perfectly, a rough pull to them, a challenge in the tone.

Kazu looks up the length of me, takes his time, lingers for a moment at my mouth, my eyes. Time bends for me, lets me feel a tiny fissure in my chest. Opening. A place to crawl into and rest. I want to fuck him right here, with Henry James and Jane Austen watching.

"She never told me your name." Kazu stands, brushes some invisible dust from his pant legs. "Honestly speaking, she never told me her name."

"I'm Margaret."

"Ashita Kazuyuki. Please call me Kazu."

"You speak English well."

"*Iya, iya.* Just I'm studying. More to learn."

"And you read."

"If time is okay."

Two high school boys in high-collared military-style uniforms appear at the end of the aisle. They take one look at us, a blue-haired gaijin and a gangster, turn on their heels and walk away quickly.

"What do you look for?" Kazu asks. His cheeks are two perfect circles of red.

What do I look for? Calm. Home. Good coffee. Happiness. Oral sex. Oblivion.

"Fiction," I say. "Something dark."

"Can I suggest?"

"Please."

"Abe Kobo *no Woman and Sand.*"

"*Woman and Sand?*"

"Story is a man is prisoner in the sand hole with the woman. He is digging every day by force. Digging, digging. He must dig or the hole will fill up. He tries to escape and can't escape. Hates the woman, then loves the woman."

"So what happens?"

"He can escape, but finally he stays in the sand hole. Digging."

"He stays for love?" I moan.

"No, for digging."

I hear the buzz of the fluorescent lights. Is it louder than normal? For some reason, in Japan, I always expect things to happen like they do in cartoons, for giant red hearts to erupt from people's chests, for connect-the-dot lines to appear in the air when lovers' eyes meet. I could swear that Kazu is reading my mind. A smile creeps onto his face. "I would like to introduce you to a good sushi shop." He says words quickly, like the rat-a-tat-tat of a machine gun. "The shop is near to here."

Kazu is a careful driver. He keeps both hands on the wheel and ignores his mobile phone that rings and bleeps and blips. The car smells new. Kazu smells like apples. I bite my fingernails and wonder where we're going.

I haven't been in a car since the night I arrived in Tokyo. A cab from the airport. In the plane, I took a sleeping pill, washed it down with three glasses of white wine, a beer, and two cognacs. Eight hours later, I woke up to the final-descent announcement, swollen feet, and a voice inside my head. The voice said, *You are such a fuckup.*

The voice is the smart me. The me that I've pushed farther and farther back into my head, the me that I've ignored, abused, neglected, subdued with pills, shushed with booze, violated with bad sex with worse men. The voice is pissed off. It wakes up before me, lies in wait, pounces on me in the rough space between sleep and waking, when I'm vulnerable.

You are nothing.

I was wedged in the middle seat between an old Japanese couple. It was two hours into the flight before I realized they were together, that I was separating them. The old woman huddled next to the window like a cornered animal. Her husband pounding whiskey in the aisle seat. They hadn't asked me to switch seats, had hardly spoken to one another. In retrospect, I remembered sad little glances that passed between them, over me. I felt a soft twinge of embarrassment, a tiny whoosh of compassion, then I quickly switched to anger. They were scared of me, scared to try to communicate with me. They were socially awkward, isolationist island people with a fear of everything different, and damned if I was moving for them. I wasn't sure whom I hated more, them or me.

You'll just wander from place to place, hoping the next plan will work out.

The plane lurched and bumped as it descended. The old lady tossed her hand across my lap and grabbed her husband's arm. He shot her a look. Embarrassment. Gave me a little series of tiny head-bows and pushed his wife's arm back.

The wandering will last but the hope won't.

The old man stared out the window as the plane breached the cloud cover. Tokyo appeared as a constellation of lights below us.

It's getting late.

The wings of the plane seesawed as the lights coalesced into a blinding neon blur. The old lady grabbed her armrests.

Wake up!

The plane was almost down. I was almost in Japan. I could start anew, couldn't I? I put my hand over the woman's. Squeezed. She flipped her hand over and squeezed back. The wheels touched down. Bump. Bump. The woman sucked in her breath. I closed my eyes. The voice shut up.

"Kazu, where are we going?"

"Ginza," he says. "Very good shop. Good sushi."

"I'm hungry."

"Food and communication, *ne*?" He looks over at me, squints. "Nervous?"

"Not really."

"Good. Never worry. Just eating. Talking. No funny business."

I laugh at his earnest expression, the way his eyes dart from the road to me to the road to me.

"What? No hanky-panky either?"

"Sushi," he says. "Beer if you want."

I smile at him. Cross and recross my legs.

Kazu looks over at me. "What is hanky-panky?"

"It's like sex, but not quite."

"Oh! Hanky-panky. Okay. *My baby does hanky-panky.* Always I wondered. What is the hanky-panky? Sex but less, *ne*? I understand."

We're stopped at the huge intersection at Ginza—land of the ten-dollar cup of tea, the thousand-dollar-a-bottle hostess bar, a never-never-land where everyone pretends the bubble never burst, where salarymen still brag that the United States is Japan's farm and Italy is its shopping mall. Through the tinted windows of Kazu's car, Ginza looks a little tired, slumping a little under the pressure of false promises.

Kazu drums his fingers on the steering wheel. "Do you *want* hanky-panky?" he asks.

The sushi shop is down a lantern-lined alleyway, tucked away from the main street. An oasis in a desert of neon. I feel like a trespasser going through the curtained entrance. The *sushiya-san*, a middle-aged man with Popeye forearms, jumps a little when he sees me, jumps a little more when he sees Kazu. They exchange a trill of words, do the requisite deep-bowing contest, and the man disappears into the back.

The room is sleek and minimal—pale wood and paper screens—everything highlighting the absence of decoration. We are the only customers. I feel like I clash with the room, that I'm at once overdressed and underdressed, shabby, awkward. Foreign. I turn to Kazu. "You know, I've lived in Japan for three months and I've never been to a love hotel." A lie, but a convenient one.

He calls out to the *sushiya-san*. Turns to me. "Takeout *ne*?"

Behind the wide, five-pronged intersection in Shibuya, steps away from the hoards of shopping teenagers and somnolent commuters, lies Love Hotel Hill, where exploitation and promiscuity are cute and charming. The hotels, with their Disneyesque exteriors, their names like Belle Chateau and Hotel Shindarella, advertise the rates on backlit signs all along the street—the three-hour screw and a shower is euphemized as a "rest," while the all-night fuckfest is a "stay." These are places where discretion is assured by the absence of human staff, where salarymen take their teenage girlfriends, housewives meet their English teachers for extra instruction, where teenage couples lose their virginity in elaborately themed rooms. Kazu seems to have a favorite hotel. He goes straight for it.

We choose our room from a machine displaying photos. Everything is automatic in these places. No front desk. No prying eyes of other humans. Just an empty lobby and a machine. No embarrassing credit card charges. Cash only, and only after the fact, through a vacuum chute in the room. Trust and deceit. Passion and mechanical efficiency. The wonderful yin and yang of the love hotel.

Kazu and I scan the photos of the rooms. There are around three dozen of them. Most look just like regular hotel rooms, except for the row of theme rooms on the fourth floor.

"Do you like swimming?" Kazu asks. "This room has a small pool."

"I like fucking."

"You are very honestly speaking girl."

"I like the Outer Space Room," I say, pointing to the photo of the space pod bed. I'm an alien. I'd like to feel weightless.

"Ii na! Good choice." He pushes a button, and a trail of tiny lights on the floor lead us to our room, to our little pod, unlocked and waiting for us.

Kazu insists on taking a bath before we get down to business.

"I'm sorry," he says, fanning himself with his hands. "I'm dirty."

He runs the bath and fusses over me, pointing out the features of the room. The television, the vending machine offering beer, green tea, and novelty condoms.

"Are you hungry?" he asks. "We can order food. Japanese noodle? Pizza? Please tell me." I like the way he says pizza—*peeza*.

"We have sushi, Kazu."

While he bathes, I get naked and watch the news. The dead girl's face appears behind the stiff, somber newscaster who trills a flurry of strange words, hardly moving his lips. The screen flickers, making it seem as if the dead girl is winking at me, her queer grin stretching back into a conspiratorial smile.

I fiddle with the music. There are one hundred and

twenty-two channels. I scan through the Japanese pop, hip-hop, rock, Euro-beat, Indian sitar, Swiss yodeling, finally settling on some U2 covers sung in Mandarin.

Kazu appears, accompanied by a whoosh of steam. The dead girl is still there—the news clip seems to go on forever—mocking us. Kazu goes to the TV and bangs at two or three buttons until the screen goes black. He stands there in his short white bathrobe and slippers.

He turns and looks at me, sitting cross-legged on the bed. Naked. Suddenly I feel undressed. Feel the atmosphere against my skin.

His face changes suddenly, from shyness through reticence to something almost cold. He smiles. I'm hot. I lie back on the bed, cross my legs, stretch my arms over my head to the silver padded headboard.

"Maybe I'm a bad man, *ne*? How do you know?" He crawls onto the bed, over me, and pushes my legs apart with his knee. His hand goes to my neck, touching me lightly, surveying me. "How do you know?"

For a moment, I imagine that the dead girl spent her last "rest" in a room like this. No, I tell myself. The body. How would they get the body out? I think of the elevator. Kazu's lips are on my chin, tracing my jawline. The elevators don't stop at other floors. They are always yours alone. His robe is open and he's on me. The best way to warm up a person with hypothermia is skin-against-skin contact. I know this. From somewhere. There must be video cameras. In the halls. The empty halls. In the lobby. The unpeopled lobby. If there weren't cameras, it would be dangerous. Privacy is an illusion—it's a door that looks like a part of a wall, behind which a middle-aged man sits and watches monitors, collects thousand-yen notes that the customers send down the vacuum chutes to pay. Privacy is always better as an idea than a reality— if we weren't being watched, excitement would ebb, panic would slide in. If we weren't being watched, what good would life be?

I put my hand on Kazu's neck, nestle my fingers into the depression at the base of his skull, pull him closer, and raise my hips against his. The bed is like an egg, split in two, the top suspended from the ceiling and lined with silvery mirrors that give distorted, wavy reflections. Kazu pins my arms back. Fear is in the room, like white noise.

Be careful, my inner voice says quietly.

Immortality is not an option, I answer back.

"It's your eyes," I tell Kazu. There is something almost feminine about them. I take the kind saucers of black-brown as a sign. This one's not going to hurt me. Not this one. Not Kazu. I keep looking at his eyes—trying to reduce the lingering fear to nothing. We're lying under the sheets, legs knotted together. I glow white next to him.

"Nani?"

"I know you're not bad from your eyes."

"Ehhh? Just black eyes. Japanese eyes. No meaning."

"Can you hand me my smokes?"

"Bad for health," he says, making a clucking sound with his tongue. *"Anata deshiou*—you have strange eyes."

"Round ones. Come on. They're on the bedside table. Hand me my lighter too."

He reaches over, plucks a Marlboro from the pack, puts it in my mouth, and flicks the lighter. Smoke curls up, hovers blue against the mirrored egg. I look down at my body. Skinny and white. Somewhere between boyish and pretty. I do not look after my pubic hair. I've always worn my puffy untrimmed bush with an absurd sense of pride, a big fuck-you to sexual mores and aesthetic salons.

Kazu takes the cigarette out of my hand and crushes it in the ashtray. "Ninety minutes. Sleeping time."

"I should go," I say. I've had sex with innumerable guys, but I've never slept with one. The intimacy of it seems inappropriate. Like giving a waiter a good-bye hug.

"You are tired," Kazu says. He brushes my bangs off my forehead. "Please."

A little argument rages in my head. My head feels heavy on the pillow. Kazu assumes the fetal position. My little voice says: *Do not spoon him. Leave now.* I turn to crawl out of the bed, but stop. Find a compromise. I lie on my side, my back against his like a mirror. The warmth of it. Sleep yanking at me. My little voice chiding me drowsily.

When I wake up, Kazu is getting dressed.

"Time," he says. His movements are sharp and precise. "Better to leave by separate ways."

"Okay." I'm searching for something to say, but my vocabulary has been reduced to pathetic clichés. *Will you call me? Can I see you again? Is everything okay?* I imagine that I'm a doll—the kind who chirps recorded phrases when you pull the cord on her back. I'm the vulnerable postcoital girl doll. Pull my string.

Kazu picks up his gold rings and slips them on his fingers one by one, grabs his mobile phone. "Your number. Please teach me," he says.

I tell him the number. He kisses me softly, on my forehead, and leaves. As he walks out, his gait changes. I can't decide whether he loosens or stiffens, but the gentleness retreats.

I breathe a little. Lie back and look at myself in the mirror, my hair splayed out like a halo on the pillow, my body compartmentalized by the various mirrors. I feel like I must be looking at someone else—that the breast here, knee there, square of white skin, outline of ribs, the foot that looks lifeless and rubbery—these parts can't be me, can't be put together into the somebody that I was this morning.

PART TWO

The Beginning of a New Era

When I get to the bar, Ines is already there, already half-cut, flirting with Jiro, who looks scared like a cornered animal. I haven't showered, and the heat of the room enlivens my just-been-fucked musk. I take a deep inhale. Ines gives me an up-and-down look as I enter. "You've been deflowered."

"Once more for old times," I say with a toss of my hair. There's an empty glass waiting for me. I fill it from the big bottle of Kirin, and marvel at the beauty of Sunday evening drinks. They are the same—the feeling is the same—in every country I've drunk in. Sunday evenings are a time when we savor each moment, turn our backs defiantly to the white crest of Monday's looming tsunami. "I don't think I was ever truly flowered. How could you tell?"

"Your makeup looks like shit. Who was it?"

"Kazu. Your shady tattooed boy." I know that Ines

won't care. She is scrupulous when it comes to nonattachment. A bedroom Buddhist. For her, desire—at least the complicated emotional kind—is the root of all suffering.

"Kazu?"

"You know."

"Is he the bald gangster or the gangster with the tight perm?"

"The bald one."

The memory clicks in. She smiles. Nods. "Oh him. He's lovely. It's not always true what they say about Japanese men, now is it?"

"An exception to every rule, I suppose." I try to look nonchalant. Hide my giddy smile behind the glass of beer.

"Fucking hell. You're not falling for him."

"Come on."

"Keep your cynicism intact, sweetie."

The first few gulps of beer are working on me. A low-grade euphoria mixed with who-gives-a-shit. "I like to stay on the low end of emotional experience," I say. "That way rock bottom is close to home."

The door opens, and a gust of wind sends bar menus fluttering in the air. Adam sneaks up behind Ines and cups her tits. She doesn't move. Takes a gulp of beer. "I'm giving you a nanosecond."

Adam's arms go into the air in mock surrender. Adam is wearing the same Chelsea football jersey he always wears. He smells like a wet ashtray and cologne. He only drinks beer and smokes dope, but he looks like a heroin addict. Grayish skin and sunken cheeks. Sad little bald patch sneaking up on him from the back. Chronically broke. Always avoiding the police. Lecherous as hell. He's the only Western male in Tokyo that I'll hang out with, the kind of guy whose luck is far overdue to run out. He, Ines, and I are like three impending head-on collisions running parallel.

"You telling me you're out of my league is it?"

"Out of your species, Adam." Ines pats the empty bar stool next to hers. "But do sit down and buy us a drink."

"Well ladies, it's your lucky day. Got me a job." Adam plunks down on the stool and smacks his hands on the bar. "Jiro my man. Set me up."

Jiro cocks his head to one side. Slowly polishes a wine glass.

"Gin and tonic IV for me and a bottle a' piss for my lady friends. Chop-chop!"

Jiro stops polishing the glass and stares at Adam.

Ines sighs. *"Jinu toniku o hitotsu to biru ippon."* She turns to Adam. "How long have you been in Tokyo, and you can't order a fucking drink in Japanese?"

"I know the language of love," he coos, flashing his gnarled yellow teeth at us. He raises his chin to me. "Marge. All right?"

Jiro puts the drinks down and tops off our beer. "The language of love is rarely understood by bartenders," I say and raise my glass to Adam. "Who the hell would hire you anyway?" Adam is of dubious visa status in Japan. He cobbles together a living by making runs to Thailand, smuggling in hash and fake designer shit. After three or four

entry stamps to Japan, when the Japanese immigration offi-
cers start to cop on to him, he throws his passport in a
washing machine in Bangkok, takes the soggy mess to the
English Embassy, and has it replaced with a brand-new one.

"Watch the language. You're speaking to a man of the
cloth now," Adam says, yellowy fingers pressed together in
prayer.

"Cheese cloth," says Ines.

"That's right. I'm a minister at New Otani Wedding
chapel. Six services every Sunday. Five grand an *I-do*."

Japanese girls love the spectacle of the Western wedding.
The meringue-like dresses, the wedding march, the quaint
little chapel, the fake minister. Any balding white-skinned
male will do.

"Inherited the job from a mate of mine— he got deported for drunk and disorderly. Called me from the airport
this morning and told me 'Get ye to the altar.' Give me a
week and I'll be shagging bridesmaids left, right, and center. I love this bloody country."

Ines reaches over, takes the giant plastic toy mallet that's
hanging on the wall, and plonks Adam over the head with
it. Her way of saying "congratulations." Jiro screws up his
face to stifle a laugh. Then, like a parent's bellowing voice
disrupting a coven of noisy children, a small earthquake
shakes the room, knocking the framed photo of John
Lennon to the floor. For a moment, the four of us are
silent. Eyes dart to eyes. Waiting. The moment is framed.
The earth stops moving. Adam rubs his head and mumbles,
"*Bloody hell.*"

Jiro does a little hop and shifts from his frozen pose, and, like a toy whose batteries have been replaced, begins to skuttle around, righting overturned bottles, picking up the menus fanned across the floor. He ticks his tongue as if to scold Mother Nature, grabs his broom, and cleans up John Lennon. His composure is betrayed only by a small blot of sweat, visible when he lifts his arm to straighten Ringo.

Ines gazes into her cleavage as if she's dropped something down there. "If you think of them like amusement park rides, they're almost fun."

"Tits?" I ask. I'm still confused. I still don't trust the walls and ceiling to stay where they are. Jiro has the bar back to normal at least—grubby but neat.

"Earthquakes. I actually quite like them now." She sighs, rests her elbows on the bar, her chin on the bridge of her hands, and winks at Jiro. "And tits too, I suppose."

"Big one coming *ne*?" Jiro says.

Ines lights two smokes and hands Jiro one. "Promises, promises."

"Fucking nutters we are—staying here." Adam's still rubbing his head. I've been hit by the plastic mallet a dozen times. It doesn't hurt. "Earthquakes. Typhoons. Fucking squat toilets."

I give Adam a little pout. "You just said you love Japan."

"Hey you should be agreeing with me, you two. Word is white girls are disappearing." He nods his head slowly. Meaningfully.

"White *girl* Adam. Just one." I'm on that drunk edge.

I'll either get belligerent or lovey-dovey. It'll happen soon.

"White slavery if you ask me. Yakuza."

"Shut the fuck up."

Belligerent it is.

"Then there's that nutter going around on a shopping bike, braining *gaijin* birds with a baseball bat."

I sigh. Adam is ruining my buzz. "You're making that up," I say.

Adam holds his palm up. "Swear it's the truth. Nearly killed an Aussie girl in Yoyogi Park."

Ines claps her hands. "What we need right now is a little smokey-smoke. Adam? Will you indulge us?"

"Bloody hell. Do you know how hard it is to get this stuff?"

"Of course we do, darling. Shall we retire to the lounge?" Ines already has Adam off his stool and halfway out the door, her hands on his back, pushing him along.

Adam turns back. "Brought it back from Bangkok." Raises his eyebrows and lowers his voice. "*Internally.*"

"Oh God," I say, pulling the sliding glass door shut. "Did you have to mention that?"

"Does it matter?"

The street is wet from a shower we missed. The slick black of the road reflecting the neon. Sidewalks buzzing with people who have somewhere to go. People with neat little lives. Paper shopping bags sheathed in plastic by attentive shop girls swing from every hand. A few moments ago, the underpinnings of the world were shifting, calling us down. I see two girls on mobile phones looking around for one another. Rising on their tippy-toes, chins high. Their eyes meet and they scurry toward each other. For a few moments, they stand face to face, fingers interlaced, still communicating through their tiny silver cells.

"No," I say. Doesn't matter.

We go around the building to a garbage-strewn alleyway and crouch by the wall. I look up at the building, which is tiled dusty-rose—eight stories tall, dotted with curtained windows, a gulag of one-room clubs with cute names. A scrawny cat with no tail slinks by, eyeing us. Adam pulls a chunk of hash from his pocket and holds the lighter to it.

"Do you ever feel like you're in a cartoon? In Japan I mean?" I'm having a *moment.*

"Fucking hell. We haven't even smoked yet." He returns to his work, arranging the little black beads on the rolling paper. "Cartoon! What the—"

"All the time," Ines answers. "What will I draw for myself tomorrow. Hmmm. Maybe an Israeli with rippling abs and a bad attitude."

"Maybe it's already drawn. The next frame. Maybe we're already drawn."

Adam puts the joint in his mouth and talks around it. "Alright Marge, I'm going to have to ask you to shut your gob. Freakin' me out already."

Somewhere water is dripping like a metronome. We smoke the joint. Our chests puff up. We speak in squeaky voices, trying to keep the smoke in. Above us, the sky is squeezing out the last remnants of day, navy blue turning black and blacker second by second. My body becomes a network of subtle sensations, tingling and buzzing. I cut and paste the feelings from part to part, enjoying the control. Paranoia is lurking there. I keep it back by staring at Adam's nose. Adam stares at Ines's chest. Ines stares at her shoes.

"Ever heard that Japanese fairy tale about the fisherman and the turtle?" Ines asks. A light rain starts to fall, and we line up—backs pressed against the wall—sheltered under a small overhang.

"So this young fisherman saves a turtle who's stuck in the mud and the turtle takes him under the sea to this fantastic castle. Pure A-list fish party. Fishy drugs and fishy martinis—"

"Mermaids?" Adam asks.

"Sure. Mermaids. Mermen. Everything. Naive little fisherboy thinks he's died and gone to heaven. He parties hard, like all night, all the next day. Mr. Turtle is all 'Stay as long as you want. Enjoy! Enjoy!' So he does, you know. He hides out. Who wants to gut fish when you can fuck an octopus? So he's looking for the loo one night and he comes upon this room where he can see his old life, his village and his family. And yeah, of-fucking-course he gets nostalgic and pathetic and tells Mr. Turtle, 'I gotta go.'

"And being the consummate host, Turtle-san gives the fisherboy a gift. A gold box that he tells him never to open. *Zenzen akimasu.* Never.

"Fisherboy says his good-byes, goes to the surface, and starts walking to his village. Everything's as dull as ever. And he's walking and walking and thinking *Hmmm, where's my house?*"

Adam has a little coughing fit, waves his hand around a bit. "Right, right—the turtle like slaughtered his family and torched his house?"

Ines slaps Adam's head. "Anyway, fisher-dork sits down under a big tree. He's used to floating around. His feet are sore, you know? He takes out the box and he can't resist—so he opens it. But there's nothing in it but a mirror. Takes him a minute to figure out it's him he's looking at—he's an old man, ancient, almost dead."

I stare at a tangled pile of abandoned bicycles. Wordless for a minute or so. The dripping is coming from both sides now, hollow and resonant. The alley feels like a cave.

Ines stands up, smoothes her hair down. "We should go dancing."

"I'm gonna go home," I say. I pray that I won't have to put up a fight. That I'll be allowed to find sleep.

Ines is stoned. Her accent—the nonspecific European snootiness of it—has softened. She almost sounds Canadian. "Don't walk," she says, pushing a ten-thousand yen note in my hand. "Anyway, I know you will. Freak. Who walks when there are cabs?"

I give Adam a peck on the cheek. He looks little brotherly with his wide red eyes, his hood pulled over his head, scraps of hair peeking out. He holds his hand against his cheek where I've kissed it and waves as I go.

After a few blocks, Aoyama Street is strangely deserted. It's like walking in an elaborate movie set. Tokyo nobody. Postapocalyptic in a calming sort of way. Pedestrian walkways crisscross above me, like shadowy arms. The streetlights go through the motions. A convenience store glows like something alive amid the concrete.

Under the cover of night, in the absence of people, Aoyama Street seems as perfectly composed as a contemplation garden. My private garden of stone, glass, and water. Mine alone to wander through. The rain-slicked streets are mine. The darkened buildings, like sleeping giants; the vacuum of silence left after the occasional car swooshes by. Mine.

I wonder what Kazu is doing.

The rain picks up. Urging me home. I tilt my head back, let it drop, heavy like a bowling ball. The raindrops look like mercury, appearing out of the inky screen, hitting my face.

I want to reach up into the weird quiet of the night, tear a strip off the black sky and wrap it around me.

Behind me, like a counterpoint to the pitter-patter of the rain, I hear the squeak of a bicycle. My ears tune into it—the whir of the wheels, water spitting up from the back tire. The slick lubricant of adrenaline guiding me, I turn abruptly at the corner, cross on the red light.

If you scream on a deserted Tokyo street, on a Sunday, in English, do you really make a sound?

The bicycle is behind me. Beside me. There's a shout—*Ki o tsukete!*— a pause for mental translation. Then relief. It's a cop.

Ki o tsukete.

Be careful.

Or literally: Take care of your feelings.

The cop smiles as he passes. Pedals away until I can no longer see his figure—just the neon stripe on the back of his jacket—until the street ahead swallows the neon stripe and I'm alone again. Panic coiled in my belly next to relief.

Fear and excitement are chemically the same. Sadness is a hair away from melancholy. Melancholy is almost pleasure, brushing against happiness. It's all the fucking same.

I'm ten. Frank's twelve. Frank says he wants a wound. A wound, he says, makes you special. People look at you differently if you're scarred. "They imagine things about you," he says. He talks about Martin MacKinnon, the boy at school who was in a car accident. His face is jigsaw-puzzled by shiny white scars. There's something happening to Frank's face. A twitchy unease has started to define his features. He's not sick yet. He's just weird.

It's been a year since Dad left—went to a convention and never came back. His shoes are still lined up in the hall closet. Sometimes I catch Mom ironing and folding his hankies, like he'll come home anytime with a cold and an old crusty handkerchief in his pants pocket, and she'll be ready for him. At first, the house was too quiet. The quiet

followed me everywhere, punctuated only by the occasional low sob from Mom's room.

Now Mom does yoga and talks a lot about her spirit
guide who is an Indian chief born a hundred years ago.
Sometimes, in the evenings, her friends come over, single
women from her office, younger than she. They wear
ribbed catsuits with zips up the front, ponchos that reek of
patchouli oil, big wiry earrings that swing from their ear-
lobes like little satellites. They smoke really thin cigarettes
and talk about finding their spiritual center. They drink
wine and hiss "He's an asshole," about Dad and other men.

I've discovered that I can spend hours and hours in my
room. Door closed. Reading young adult novels about teen
pregnancy and lithe ballet-dancing teenagers with eating
disorders and doe eyes. I can hide away for entire weekends
and no one notices at all. My room. My kingdom.

Frank finally decides that he'll cut one of his pinky fingers off. He plans it for a whole week, going through the
knives in the kitchen and finding the sharpest one, figuring
out the best joint to slice at. Just the tip isn't dramatic
enough, but too close to his palm and he might sever a ten-
don. He'll drop the finger down the garbage disposal so
they can't reattach it.

Frank chooses a Sunday afternoon when Mom will be
sleeping in front of the TV. He prepares a bag of ice and
positions me at the doorway to scream for help. We get our
stories straight.

"We were hungry so we decided to have bagels and

peanut butter but the bagels were all frozen and the knife just slipped. Okay?" He's twitchy with excitement.

I'm scared but I say, "Okay."

Frank smiles, picks up the knife. "It's time," he says.

The scream comes out so fast and shrill Frank drops the knife. "Mom!"

Frank gives up on the wound idea. For a week he looks at me with a mixture of sadness and contempt.

"You can still be special," I tell him. "You're smart."

"That's not the way things work," he tells me.

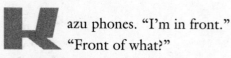azu phones. "I'm in front."

"Front of what?"

"Apartment."

I look out my window. There's his car. A big gray Mercedes with tinted windows. An old lady pulling a shopping caddy eyes the car sideways. I imagine Kazu behind the wheel. Phone to his ear. Connected to me. My pulse quickens.

"I'm coming," I tell him. I should wait thirty seconds. Feign indifference. Slap on some lipstick. But I take off down the stairs. Take two at a time. Step into my shoes and make for the car.

"Western woman," Kazu says. "Very fast."

"So they say." I lean over and cup his face in my hands. Take his upper lip between mine and suck it a little. Kazu closes his eyes like a cat does when you rub its ears. I let go of his face and examine the books on his lap. Japanese-English dictionary. English-Japanese dictionary. Electronic dictionary. *Your New Western Girlfriend: A Guide for the Asian Man.* The latter sounds like an instruction manual for a blowup doll. It has a misty photograph of a girl in a sundress walking through a meadow, blond hair lifted off her shoulders by a breeze.

"You've got to be joking," I say.

"Preparation," Kazu says. He gestures at me strangely. Knuckles against knuckles.

"Huh?"

"Seat-o-belt-o," he says. An earnest sort of smile. "I like to drive rapidly."

Kazu rolls off me. The Japanese-themed room is bare except for a futon and low table. "Feeling. How?"

"Good," I say, fumbling for my smokes.

"No," Kazu takes me by the chin and turns my face to him. "Please. I want detail. How?"

"Like," I light a smoke, stare up at the ceiling, "like I'm dissolving."

"Eh?"

"Like I'm less me."

Kazu grabs the cigarette and takes a drag. "Honestly speaking," he says, "I am married man."

My mouth opens. Air escaping a pricked balloon. "I don't care."

t's "Make a Scene!" day at Air-Pro, when we role-play challenging airplane scenarios— screaming babies, belligerent businessmen, terrorists, vegans. I think of my mother, the way she'd say "Don't make a scene!" when Frank got weepy in the meat section of the supermarket.

It's hard for me to concentrate at work. The role-playing helps. It always helps to be someone other than me. Today I am the drunk old pervert businessman.

We arrange the chairs to approximate the cabin of a jumbo jet, and tape signs around the room—"cockpit" on the whiteboard, "galley" on the podium, "emergency exit" on the door.

The first recruit is Nami, a fair-faced girl with a mouth full of braces. Her head is perpetually turned at an angle, as though the world was forever presenting her with quandaries. Nami stands in the corner with a chirping coven of nervous recruits, smoothing down her fitted blue skirt compulsively. I know she is terrified of me, like all the rest, but I no longer get a perverse satisfaction from it, from the panicky little bows, the suspended conversations as I pass by. I feel like a reluctant sadist.

Ms. Nakamura claps her hands, and we take our places. I slouch down in my seat, slip into character. I see myself in a crumpled, ill-fitting suit, potbelly spilling over my belt, a salt-and-pepper mustache adorned with almond skins and spittle. From the depths of my lipid-clogged heart, an angry sort of lust rises. I clear my throat and push the imaginary bell on my armrest.

"Dewars!" I scream. It's not my voice. There's a collective gasp from the other recruits sitting rigidly in economy class.

Nami teeters down the aisle, steadying herself on the backs of chairs as if there was turbulence.

"Yes, sir?" she squeaks. "How can I be of assistance?" Her lip quivers.

"Assistance!" I scream. "Whiskey, girl! I need whiskey!"

"Yes sir!" Nami makes it to the podium, pours an invisible drink, twisting the cap back on the imaginary bottle, with undue care. She takes a deep breath, her chest puffing up like a little chicken breast and deflating with a whoosh of air.

"Your whiskey, sir." She leans down from the waist, hands me the drink. She smells of vanilla and powder.

"Ever seen a trouser snake?" I ask.

"Pardon me, sir?"

I make a grab for her ass and get a handful of buttock-enhancing padding. Screaming, Nami darts out the exit, clip-clopping down the hallway to the washroom. Ms. Nakamura claps furiously, two fingers against her palm. "So real! So real!" she says. I down the imaginary whiskey in one gulp, pull my hand across my mouth, and think about ritual suicide.

On Nami's "Make a Scene!" report, I write: "Your smile and posture were lovely. You were handling the situation beautifully right up until you depressurized the cabin, killing all of the passengers and crew." I sign it "Satan" in an illegible scrawl.

In the lobby, I see Madoka, sitting hunched over, reading a flight attendant magazine and sucking on her bottom lip. I sit down next to her, and she jumps. Fumbles with the magazine. Concealed behind the facade of *International Stewardess* is a thick *manga*—spy-girls with catsuits and guns. Secret missions and round cantilevered breasts. Madoka looks at me guiltily. I click my tongue at her. Give her a wink. The compassion I feel for her is like a whoosh of warm air. It shocks me.

Nakamura appears out of nowhere and says, "Madoka-san! Time to learn how to sit." She claps her hands. Smiles wickedly.

I place my hand on Madoka's shoulder. "God be with you," I tell her.

The Log Cabin Room looks like a sauna with a vibrating bed, plastic fireplace, and a leopard-spot sofa. Kazu strolls around the room. Opening a drawer. Inspecting the radio console. Sitting down on the sofa and then getting up again. He looks a little disappointed. "*Canada mitain?*"

"No Canada's a bit different."

He walks around me once and then comes up behind me, wraps one arm around my waist. Pulls my hair off my neck and kisses me.

"No perfume," he says.

"Not until they make one that smells like a dog's paw."

"Never mind. I like your smell."

We make our way over to the bed. Fumble with clothes. Bodies tense. I look over to the alarm clock. Calculate the time remaining on the room.

"You have appointment?" Kazu asks.

"No. You?"

"I make the schedule. Today I schedule Margaret."

"What exactly is it that you do?" I ask.

"Do?"

"Your job."

"Businessman," he says.

"Salaryman?"

"Similar. Yes."

"You sell things?"

"Helping selling things. Yes."

"Do you have an office?"

"Margaret-chan. We Japanese have a saying."

"Yes?"

"Stay quiet, learn more."

"Have you ever cut someone's finger off?"

Kazu sits up. The muscles at his jawline tense and shudder, like a small animal stirring under his skin. I wait for something. Behind his stare, I think I can see decisions being made. Options run through.

"Cutting finger is for apology."

"Like. . . I'm sorry. Here's my finger?"

"Yes."

I offer up my hand to him. Run it across his forehead, down his cheek. When I go to touch his mouth, he snatches up my fingers. Holds them tight in a little bundle. "Questions finish," he says and puts my hand on his cock. I nestle my body against his. Blood rushes to my crotch. I tense against him. He moves down. A shudder runs through me at his touch. It's building in me. A room filling with gas. Waiting for the spark. The French call it "petit mort." Little death. He reaches his arm under me, lifts my body up to his mouth.

Lying in the sweet vulnerability of finished lovemaking. A dangerous time. I promise myself never to ask the question again. But I always do. An uncontrollable compulsion to rub off my patina of self-respect in five monosyllables. "Why do you like me?" I ask. Kazu squints at me, and in a flash I run through some of the more tragic responses from the past. *You live next door. My girlfriend is really fat. I'm lonely. I have no idea.*

"Because I saw you sucking finger." He demonstrates with his thumb in his mouth.

"Thumb," I tell him.

"Thumb. In the Space Room, I watched you. It makes my heart calm. Also I like a challenge." He pulls me on top of him. "Difficult to make you happy I think."

Try. Please.

We lie there. Nose to nose. I've grown to love the lines of the Japanese face. The way the nose doesn't jut out of the face but slinks down. I feel so pointy next to him, with my aggressive facial features. Wonder how he could choose me over the subtle beauty of a Japanese woman.

"What's she like?" I ask. "Your wife?"

He pulls back from me, rolls over, and lights a smoke from my bedside pack. I've never seen him smoke. "Difficult," he says. "She is—" He takes out an electronic dictionary—it's weird how every Japanese person seems to have one handy. "One moment please." He punches something in and turns the tiny speaker toward me. "Psych-o-path," the electronic voice sounds out. He closes the dictionary and slips it in his shoulder bag. "Also she likes brand goods too much—Prada *to ka*, Gucci *to ka*."

"What would she do if she knew about me?"

Kazu drags on the cigarette like a seasoned smoker. Like someone in a black-and-white movie. Smoking as an extension of speaking. A form of punctuation.

"Please don't think about that." He exhales. Period. Full stop.

like to walk home from the love hotels. Through the little streets they are tucked away on, toward the bustling train stations, the chaos of the intersections. I like the hotels around Shinjuku Station the best. I walk around the monstrosity of the station—something like three million people passing through it every day. One million. Three million. Twelve million. It's all incomprehensible. From the outside, it doesn't look like a building at all. Sprawling six city blocks. Cobbled together over the years as more train lines were constructed. Impossible to navigate from the inside. From certain angles it looks evil. I've always had a soft spot for the place. When I first arrived in Tokyo, I couldn't stop walking around Shinjuku Station. It wasn't just that I was lost, which I was, but I felt as if I'd found my place. The endless anonymous concourse. It had everything I needed. There was coffee and food. I could light up a smoke wherever I pleased. There were no windows, but I've never had much use for sunshine. If I walked long enough, the tunnels led me to department-store food halls, where girls in fifties-style cafeteria uniforms handed me strange morsels on toothpicks. Gifts for the weary traveler. There was always a crowd to be swept up into. I imagined being lifted off my feet, dragged by the shoulders of salarymen and schoolgirls to somewhere I couldn't fathom.

I walk along the outside at street level. Two levels of pedestrian walkways hug the side of the building. Commuters and students, shoppers and girls handing out packets of tissues emblazoned with adverts—*Hai! Dozo, onegaishimasu!* I'm in a daze. Freshly fucked. Happy and buzzing.

On the second level of walkways, I see her. She stands out from the other walkers. She's tall. Her blond hair catching the sun. Her profile. The nose. Something else. Something that tells me it's her. She's moving fast. I start to run. Look ahead half a block to the staircase to her level. I'm running. I seem to have a sense. How to get through the people traffic. Like I'm in a video game and I'm winning.

I look up again. It's her. I know it's her. The dead girl. Alive.

I keep running. Faster. The moment closing in on me. Like sex. Running toward something and away from something simultaneously. I make it to the staircase. Take the steps two by two. I want to look at her. Hold her by the shoulders and have a look at her. The eyebrows. The wicked arch of them. The light spray of freckles. The eyes that have watched me in all my dark moments. I make it to the top. My legs hurt. They won't cooperate. When I stumble, catching the edge of the last step with the heel of my palm—concrete against skin— the gaggle of schoolgirls appears. Sailor tops and blue skirts. In front of me, like a wall. Making noises like birds or machines, or machines meant to sound like birds. I lose sight of the lost girl. Gone into the station or down the stairs. Gone.

I'm fourteen. Frank's sixteen.

Frank is slowly retreating from the world. I'm growing boobs. And getting skinny. It happens over the summer vacation before grade ten. I grow two inches. There's a heat wave. Maybe I sweat the fat off. My chest swells like bread in an oven. I lie in bed, survey my body under the tent of the cotton sheet. I can see the outline of my ribs. It makes me think of greyhounds.

Sometimes I lock the bathroom door and strike poses. Sometimes I wink at myself. Lean into the mirror, lips parted for a kiss. Mom says I'm blooming. I smell funny. Like fruit going bad.

In phys-ed class the next year, the girls eye me suspiciously. I feel like I've broken some code of conduct. We're learning to dive, but I can't do it. It seems wrong to leap into the hands of gravity that way. For amusement. For course credit.

The boys start to notice me, too.

I'm kept after school to learn to dive.

"Keep your chin tucked in," barks the teacher. "Keep your legs together."

In science class, we make little models of DNA molecules. It's like a map, the teacher tells us. Everything we are is mapped out in our genes. He has the gene for red hair. That's recessive. It's rare. It's why family members share traits. It's why some diseases run in families.

I wonder what's mapped in me. The crazy gene. The loser gene. My hair is the color of straw. I wonder if that gene is rare.

I get paired up with Tony Varda. I was taller than he last year, but he's grown. At first, I'm nervous. Each movement, each facial expression seems forced and awkward. Then I begin to watch him. The thin layer of sweat on his forehead. The jerkiness of his hands. The way he can't look at me. I let my eyelids go heavy. Look out from under them and curl my mouth up into a half-smile. He fumbles with the little plastic sticks and balls. "Here. Let me," I say.

It happens like that. Like instinct. I know how to torture boys. Exquisitely. Maybe it's mapped in me.

We go up in one of the little elevators in one of the hundreds of narrow buildings in Asakusa. These entertainment buildings are everywhere in Tokyo. Along all the main streets. They look like dingy office buildings, except for the neon and chaotic signage. In the elevator, I look at the backlit building guide. Forty-eight little bars and restaurants and karaoke places in one little six-story building on a street with hundreds of little buildings, in a city with hundreds of streets like this.

"Japanese pancake," Kazu says.

"Huh?"

He points to something written in kanji on the building guide. "For eating. *Okonomiyaki* restaurant."

"Oh, okay."

The hallways in these buildings are always dodgy. The various odors of all the bars and restaurants seeping into the corridors. Melding into an aroma peculiar to these places—something like old cigar smoke and dirty underpants. Kazu's mobile rings, and he nods at me in apology, holds his palm out to me like telling a dog to stay and wanders down a few feet away for privacy.

I look at my watch. Almost nine. Dip one hip down an inch or two and sulk. A door flies open, and two salarymen carrying a third by his armpits stagger out. A wistful country song accompanies them. Then three Thai hostesses. Lurid pink lips. Soft hips compressed in spandex dresses. The salaryman being carried looks like he's going to vomit. Everyone is yelping. Some money is exchanged. Some bowing is done.

I walk to the end of the hall and duck out the fire escape for air. There is no air. The exterior of the building is tented by enormous vinyl sheeting, stretched over the frame of the fire escape, advertising beer and loan sharks and hairspray. I imagine a fire breaking out. The advertisements melting in the heat, suffocating the revelers in the building with toxic fumes. The fire spreading to the adjacent buildings, consuming city blocks, eating the city like a neon Dresden. The thought of it raises my pulse. A mixture of fear and morbid glee.

I yank at the side of one of the vinyl sheets, pull it aside like a curtain, and peek out at the street. Three squat men in white uniforms carry an enormous fish as big as two of them put together. I can hear their grunts of effort over the noise of the street. They pass a group of Japanese hostesses. Puffy down jackets over their slinky dresses, calling out to passing salarymen. Pretty girls with pain in their faces. When the fish carriers pass, the girls call out to them, too. *Gambarimasu!* Do your best.

"Are you okay?" Kazu asks. He's standing in the fire escape doorway. A look of real concern on his face. I watch him for a second. Behold this *look*. I don't want Tokyo to burn down.

"Yes," I say and take his hand.

The *okonomiyaki* place is full of wood and smells like smoke and onions. A few groups of three or four people are scattered in the booths that line the room. The comforting din of it relaxes me. We find a booth in the back. The center of the table is a griddle. Kazu switches it on and signals for the waiter.

"Have you tried Japanese pancake?" Kazu asks.

"Only from the *konbini*."

Kazu waves his hand. "Convenience-store kind is not so good."

The waiter plunks down a large bottle of beer and two squat glasses. He and Kazu speak to each other in clipped, guttural Japanese. The kind that men use together in comfortable situations. They share an abbreviated little laugh, and the waiter disappears.

"Why did you come to Japan?" Kazu asks me.

"International human friendship," I say with a smile.

"Serious answer," Kazu says without a smile.

"To be alone."

"In Japan? Alone?"

"It's an easy place to be alone."

Kazu watches me for a moment. Picks up the beer bottle and pours me some. After he puts it down, I reciprocate. The beer foams up a little and spills onto the table.

"When I was a young man—sixteen, seventeen—" Kazu tells me, "I wanted to be a chef. I was apprentice at a big restaurant. Very high-level Japanese cooking. Every day I was in a small kitchen." He makes a chopping gesture. "Maybe ten or twelve other cooks. So close our elbows always are touching elbows. Six A.M. to maybe ten o'clock nighttime. Six days a week." The waiter pours the batter onto the table and Kazu shoos him away, pokes at the blob of batter, squid bits, and cabbage, perfecting its shape. "After working every day, do you know what I had to do? Part of Japanese culture? I had to take a bath with the other cooks. Giant round bath. All together." Kazu unclips his cuff links. Small diamonds that might look garish on anyone else. Rolls up his sleeves. His shirt is immaculately pressed. I imagine his wife leaning over an ironing board, dressed in Dior and stiletto heels. "It is not easy to be alone in Japan," he tells me.

"So why didn't you become a chef?"

He sniffs, offers me a shake of his head for an answer. "About alone in Japan. Yes. Now I'm thinking my grandfather did it. I remember now. After retirement he walked to the sea every day. One hour from the house. Every day he sat in the same place, on a big rock, and smoked tobacco all day. His father was a fisherman. My grandfather, forty years post office. After that, watching the sea. Sitting on one rock. Smoking and watching from sunrise until nighttime. Alone." Kazu's eyes become glassy for a moment. Nostalgia taking hold. Then he comes back. "My family was thinking he was weak of mind. Fault of age."

"Did you think so?"

"In truth I wanted to try it. When I was a boy. Sea watching."

"Go with him?"

"No," he says. "Alone. Different rock." He takes a smoke out of my pack, but doesn't light it. Just turns it in his hands. "Tell me what happened to you in Canada."

I adjust my posture. Shift my butt back on the bench and straighten my back. "I saw the white girl who's missing. The one on the posters. At Shinjuku Station."

"Different person, I think. Answer my question please."

"No. I recognized her."

"Many blond-hair gaijin in Tokyo, I think." He reaches over and touches my hair. "Example. Margaret."

"I know it was her. I have a feeling."

"Ah," he says. "Feeling."

"Maybe she's hiding out or something."

Kazu prods the bubbling batter with the spatula. "I don't think so."

"Maybe she's in trouble."

"You ought to forget this." In one swift movement, Kazu flips the pancake, but it's too soon. Batter oozes out the side. "She's dead," he says.

I want to say *It could have been me on the posters.* "No. It was her I saw," I tell him.

"Use your brain. This happens." He scoops up the fractured *okonomiyaki* into a little hill in the center of the table and signals for the waiter. "We'll start again new pancake."

Start again. Impossible. "Don't bother," I tell Kazu. "I'm not hungry anymore."

I go to stand up, but Kazu reaches across the table and grabs my wrist. "You need food. Sit down."

We sit there quietly for a few minutes. Sipping beer and staring through one another. Both of us lost in the past. "*Natsukashii,*" Kazu says absently. A word I don't understand. But I like the sound of it. The sibilant gush of it. I repeat it back to him. *Natsukashii.* Feel the uncanny joy of the alien. He nods at me.

"Is your grandfather still alive?" I ask.

"Dead," Kazu says.

I'm fifteen. Frank's seventeen. Mired in the theater of high school. Anyone with eyes can tell. All the fat kids look alike. Faces somewhere in the middle of their cheeks. Lips squished up into grotesque puckers. The popular girls, too. Carbon copies. They all have shiny hair and noses like dolls'. Two expressions. Evil and vacant. Ditto for the weirdo loser intelligentsia. Bad posture. Bad eyesight. A penchant for disturbingly violent doodling. Frank falls into the latter category. I'm in limbo. "You just haven't found your niche," Mom tells me. The way she says "niche" rhymes with "bitch."

Frank and I avoid each other scrupulously at school. I almost despise him when I see him in the halls. His hunched-over walk, eyes darting side to side. Frank is like a car crash in slow motion. I wince and wait for the crush of impact. Finally begin to turn away. Wish it was just over with.

"So," I say to Tony Varda. "Sometimes my mom goes away on business."

"Yeah?" I can hear his labored breathing, the way he's holding the receiver too close to his face. I think for a minute that I ought to tell him the receiver harbors bacteria. That he'll turn into a crater-face if he keeps pressing the phone into his cheek that way. I wonder why guys are so repulsive. Why I like them despite it.

"You could stay over," I say. Something happens to the words on their way out. In my throat, they're jittery, unnatural. But they emerge brazen. I feel vulgar. It feels good.

"Yeah?"

"Can you say something else?"

"Huh?"

"Something other than yeah?"

He snorts.

"Don't you want me?" Vulgar retreats. Pushed out by pathetic.

"Yeah," he says with a puff of breath into the mouthpiece.

My stomach is twisting. It's in my throat. *Say "I like you." Say "You're so pretty."*

"I've gotta go bad. Meet me after school tomorrow," he says. "By the creek."

I put down the phone and imagine the two of us lying on a bed of red leaves, canopy of trees over us. Tony touching me like something in a museum. Something that might crumble at his touch. In my fantasy, Tony does not have white spittle collected at the corners of his mouth. In my fantasy, I am not a loser.

Frank comes downstairs, into the kitchen. "What's wrong?" I ask him. He's sweating. His hands are making claw-like movements under his chin.

"Okay. Okayokayokay." He sits down. "Where's Mom?"

"I dunno—"

"Is she home?" he screams. "Okay. This is it. It sounds crazy, but this is it. This thing—this guy was in my room."

"What guy?"

"He was short. More than short. He was— he was a troll or an elf or a gnome or something. I'm not entirely sure of the difference. If I were to venture a guess in spite of my ignorance, I'd have to say he was a gnome. And he was like prismatic. A rainbow gnome. He was there and gone so fast."

"Frank—"

"Don't tell Mom."

"But—"

"Oh what's happening? What's happening?"

"Maybe it was a dream," I say. I touch his shoulder.

Frank grabs my hand. "It wasn't a dream." He says the words slowly, deliberately. The neighbor's dog lopes in the kitchen door. Smiling. Looks at the two of us and licks his chops.

"It was the beginning of a new era," Frank says.

On mock-interview day at Air-Pro Stewardess Training Institute, Ms. Nakamura instructs me, "In classroom, firm but kind. In mock interview, only firm."

Ms. Nakamura is in some special mock-interview day get-up. Her hair is pulled back so tightly I can see that she's had to pencil in her eyebrows an inch below where the shaved- off ones are. Her normal little tight suit replaced by a white shift dress with a dramatically long white coat worn precariously over her bony shoulders, like a cape. It makes me nervous to look at her. As though at any moment laser beams might shoot out of her eyes and burn me up.

"You will conduct the interviews with Mr. Shawn from head office." Nakamura starts to swivel around on her high heels. "Mr. Shawn!"

Mr. Shawn appears in the doorway of the interview

room. He has a dimple in his chin, pasty skin, and eyes set so close you are forced to focus on the dimple to avoid going cross-eyed.

He walks over stiffly, as though his arms will not rest comfortably by his side. "Shawn," he says. "Head office."

Before I can introduce myself, Nakamura tells me that Mr. Shawn is "very tough cookie" and shoos us into the interview room to prepare.

"It's a piece of cake, really," Shawn tells me, handing me the interview sheet. "I ask the questions in blue. The pink ones are yours. We go back and forth."

I look at the sheet. Shawn's questions are things like "Tell me about your international experiences" and "What current affairs are you interested in?" I have to ask things like "How do your parents feel about your career goal?" and "What would you say to a passenger who hands you a dirty diaper to dispose of?"

Mr. Shawn leans back in his chair, gazes out through the two-way mirror at the recruits standing stiffly. "Shit, I love my job. These girls are prime."

"Prime what?"

"We have a joke at the head office. All of the cabin-related questions can be correctly answered with 'Give him a blow job.'"

I just stare at him. Sitting slackly. Cross-legged. His socks don't match. Above the socks, a grotesque patch of pale, sparsely haired skin is visible.

"You know, like, 'What would you do if an obviously intoxicated passenger asks for another drink?'" His eyes resemble two pissholes in the snow. "Give him a blow job! Get it?"

The first recruit performs perfectly. Her face frozen into an expression equally wistful and fanatically ambitious. At moments, during the interview, as she details her love of animals and the novels of Milan Kundera, her desire to provide superior cabin service and "experience the architectural delights of many countries," I almost envy her. Her single-minded purpose. Her innocence. I try to remember back to the time, around the age of eight, when I wanted to be a veterinarian. How I'd hover past bedtime with library books devoted to the profession. Dogs in tiny casts, horses giving birth in grotesque detail. Somehow these girls had retained some of that wonder that I struggle to recall.

Although she never once answers her cabin questions with offers of oral sex, Mr. Shawn gives her a nine out of ten, and, with a creepy stare, compliments her on the way she holds her body.

Mock-interview day passes like a skipping record. Beautiful girl after beautiful girl. I begin to champion them, these specimens of the unjaded. Firm becomes firm but kind, becomes just kind. *My parents support me in my career choice.* Eager to escape the hamster wheel of office work and domesticity. *I'm interested in the exciting world of aviation.* To stay in hotels in strange cities, like an expense-paid pajama party. *I want to share with the world the culture of Japan.* Have sex with big men with big cocks. *I would suggest to frightened passenger that he take deep breaths and read the in-flight magazine.* Maybe I'm not so different from them—we all want to fly away.

On the way out, Mr. Shawn shakes my hand. "Well," he says. "Don't worry. It will get easier." I lean into the handshake and call him an impotent little weasel boy. He deflates suddenly. Wide eyes and pursed lips. Foreign woman. Cryptonite to the Western supermale in Japan. He reflates. Nods, "Oh, good one. Ha ha. You had me there for a sec." I give him a firm little squeeze on the shoulder. In the elevator, I share a high five with two of the recruits, make it to the street, breathe in steam from a noodle-vendor's cart and something more unusual—the rarefied air of international human friendship.

And then Kazu doesn't call. A day. Three days. Four days. A week. You feel yourself deflating. Losing substance. He never gave you his phone number. You are in Siberia. In a flimsy hut. The wind howling around you.

Funny how it happens. How things change. You tell yourself that love is for other people. People with soft hearts and fixed addresses. You believe your heart pumps blood. That's it. That sex is a need— like food and water— that people who make it into something else watch too many romantic comedies.

Intimacy is a word with eight letters.

A word with a sly hiss to it.

But then it begins, like love affairs do, with a chance meeting, and then a raw empty something needing to be sated, something you didn't notice before. But suddenly it squawks like a hungry bird, day and night, refusing to be ignored. You love and revile it, this sore shrieking something. Or is it nothing? Or everything? It doesn't matter. It's yours. It's you.

Suddenly you are a walking cliché. The sum total of every love song penned. Even the Japanese ones, with the words you can't catch—you recognize yourself in the fragile thrum in the singer's voices. Life is suddenly so banal compared with the transcendence of the love-hotel tryst. When the walls heave and huddle closer, you ride the Yamanote loop line around Tokyo. Round and round again, until your butt gets sore, until you feel like you could stay there forever, looking at the advertisement with a geisha brandishing a power drill. After two or three hours, you start to wonder if the get-from-point-A-to-point-B function of the subway might be a complete ruse. You start to suspect that maybe everyone—the pregnant woman in her cutesy bib dress and bucket hat, the sullen teenager carrying her six-hundred-dollar handbag and touching and retouching her lip gloss, the salaryman sleeping, mouth agape, in the corner seat—maybe they are all going nowhere. Just riding the train to kill time. Kill memory. To enjoy the spectacle of anonymity. The thought is a temporary buoy. You stay as long as the imagined collective ennui entertains you. You stay until the light changes, the salarymen and schoolgirls disappear, and the train is filled with fashionable twentysomethings, so scrupulously cool, so effortlessly hip you want to smash their faces in. Best to leave, when the violent impulses start.

• • •

You get a bottle of wine. After half a bottle, the *need* is diluted. You start to feel less like a detached Siamese twin. More like a garden-variety fuckup. Pick up your mobile phone and tell it, *You are not my master*. Drink some more and wait for Ines.

"Darling," she says as she flings the door open, "I've procured love pills."

Perfect.

Ines is in her underwear, applying mascara. Mouth open. Bent over at the waist. I'm looking at her butt. It's honey brown.

"Where'd you get the tan?" I ask.

"Granny. She was Métis or Tunisian. One of the two." Ines stands up, solemnly inspects her handiwork in the mirror. "She's dead now."

I look down at my legs. I'm so white I'm nearly blue. "Tell me a secret," I say and fold my legs under me like a hen on her eggs.

"There was a time, not so long ago, when certain Celine Dion songs could make me weep and sway."

"Come on."

"Okay, Ines isn't my real name."

"That I knew."

"Your turn."

"I think I'm destined to go nuts."

"That I knew."

"Seems to happen to everyone around me. Except my mom—she went—" I pause, "New-Agey."

"Same difference."

"I just wish I could fast-forward to old age. Youth is like being in an airplane in a tailspin."

"Enjoy the ride, gorgeous." Ines slips a shapeless tube of black fabric over her head, transforms it into a slinky dress. She sighs at her reflection in the mirror, as if being beautiful had become banal, tiresome. "I'm going to wear outrageous hats when I'm old."

"I'm going to collect commemorative teaspoons and figurines."

"Date men with walkers and fat life-insurance policies."

"Dye my hair blue."

"It's already blue sweetie."

"See? I'm already halfway there. Bring on the knick-knacks!"

"Let's go, huh?"

"Oh God, not let's go."

"It doesn't matter where we are," Ines steps into her kitten-heeled mules, drags me off the bed and links elbows with me. "Just that we are there."

I make a low growling sound in my throat. "Let's go," I mutter.

Bar Let's Go is a place where no one thinks they belong but everyone ends up. If you go to Bar Let's Go, staying sober is not an option. It's a very good idea to arrive intoxicated, otherwise you'll have to down several martinis in quick succession to blunt the reality of Bar Let's Go.

You are in a room that, if bathed in light, would resemble a government office stripped of the desks and chairs: four walls, no character, purpose-built, a temple to the god of wretched excess and bad design. Pass through the doors, pay the thousand-yen cover charge, and buy into the myth that good things happen when we poison ourselves in a dark, smoky room full of people we vaguely despise.

Pimply white boys from Minneapolis or Mississauga revel in their newfound pulling power. Japanese office ladies sip pastel drinks and troll for a bit of strange before they consign themselves to domestic servitude.

All I can hear, all I can sever from the confused din is talk of the missing girl. Snippets of theories, conjecture, morbid fascination. *I heard she's in Thailand. In hiding. In a cult. In a bodybag.* Ines and I plant ourselves at a table and suck on martinis, waiting for pill-boy. *She's not the first to vanish.* The pills better arrive soon. I'm starting to shrink away again. *The cops don't care.* The missing girl has made us, the melanin-deficient diaspora, feel special by virtue of our connection with something tragic. Everyone seems to have shared a drink with the dearly departed, been a schoolmate, a coworker, had a friend who knew someone who sat across from her on the train. Everybody wants to be a survivor of something appalling—the person at the epicenter of the earthquake who walks away without a scratch, walks away with a story to tell again and again at dinner parties, a story to imbue their lives with an aura of luck and immortality. Tragedy makes excellent chitchat.

"Okay Marge. It looks like your face is melting. I insist you have fun."

"I'm in one of my funks. I'm sorry."

"Play the worst-case-scenario game."

"Tell me how."

"It's like this. When I was in high school I went to a house party. After the cops bust the thing up, everyone starts piling into cars to go to a bar. I want to be in Trevor Spence's little red MG, but Sadie Trembley beats me to it— wily little bitch. Short version, the stud runs the car into a tree. Rumor is she was sucking him off—I mean, how cliché. Sadie goes through the windshield face-first. Sixteen metal pins and four operations later she still looks like Frankenstein."

"Frankenstein's monster. Frankenstein was the mad scientist."

"Whatever. Point is. Worst-case scenario I could be living with my mother, writing technical manuals and avoiding mirrors. But I'm here in a tragic club in Tokyo. With *you*, darling."

"Ah."

"Makes me feel better every time."

"Feed on the suffering of others to pump myself up."

"*Exactement.*"

nes disappears into the ether and strobe lights, and I'm left perched on my stool to contemplate the ashtray. The room—the crowd—is all shyness and reticence. The calm before the come-on. A few tourists in khaki shorts and Teva sandals storm the dance floor, jerking about robotically, exchanging knowing looks. The rest of the people, still huddled in nervous little tribes, look upon the tourists with disdain, waiting for the dance floor to thicken so they, too, can jerk robotically—in relative anonymity, shrouded in bodies.

A Japanese girl in white knee-high platform boots, white lipstick, and eyeliner to match bounds across the empty dance floor. The mouth-breathing white boys stop talking, slack-jawed as white-boots clops toward the tables, her skirt riding up on her little thighs until it's little more than a wide belt. Her hands are in the air in some sort of high-speed perversion of the queen's wave. She's not so much sexy as unknowingly hemorrhaging sex. No one trying to be sexy would run that way.

Then, through the clamor of heavy breathing and bass beat, I hear my name. Or a high-pitched butchering of my name. *Mah-ga-let!* The bouncing, squealing girl is bouncing toward me, squealing my name. I squint at her. She looks vaguely familiar. And frightening. Her head seems huge as she trips, recovers, lunges toward me. It's Madoka Wakiyama. The new recruit. Looking very unstewardessy.

Madoka sucks in air, shakes her fingers as if they are on fire and she needs to put them out. She points at her mouth, gasping, holds up a finger to signal me to wait. Madoka clearly has something important to say. I wait. After one final inhalation, tears forming at the corners of her white-lined eyes, she comes out with it.

"Margaret-sensei—" breath—"why so cute you are?"

Before I can ponder the question, compose an answer, Ines is back from somewhere, back with a smile on her face, back with the pills.

"Madoka, Ines. Ines, Madoka."

"Ehhh?" Madoka says, stroking Ines's hair. "*Kirei!* Beautiful."

Ines takes Madoka's hand and places it on the table. "Paws off the hair, please."

"You're beautiful and I'm cute," I say. "Story of my life."

"Cute has more currency in Japan, darling."

"Cute ages badly. Anyway, let's get happy, huh?"

Madoka is nodding her head, turning her chin to face whoever's talking. She has the glassy-eyed, falsely rapt expression of someone who hasn't a fucking clue what's being said.

"Who's the go-go dancer?"

"Madoka. She's one of my stewardess students."

"She's very keen."

"Yep."

"Maybe we should give her a pill."

"That's a bad idea." I imagine the most illicit thing Madoka's ever done is drinking beer straight from the bottle. "A very bad idea."

"Those are my favorite kind." Ines turns to Madoka. Holds out a pill. "This is a drug, darling. An illicit substance. If you get caught with it, you'll be hauled down to the police station and your entire family will be shamed for perpetuity. You won't lose face. You'll lose face, head, neck, and shoulders. But you'll feel lovely for the next little while. How about it?" Ines babbles something in Japanese, something that shocks Madoka's lips into an O. Madoka squints, lolls her head, and before I can stop her, scoops the pill from Ines's hand and pops it in her mouth.

"Fuck, Ines."

"She made an informed decision."

"Now you have to take care of her, you realize."

"Oh shush. Take your pill, down your drink, and let's boogie."

"Boogie!" Madoka says.

. . .

After the pills are taken, the booze is downed, Ines and Madoka disappear to the dance floor. I opt to sulk and observe the prickly sensations under my skin. In order to dance without feeling unbearably self-conscious, I have to be under the influence of a substance that either obliterates my ego or expands it to gargantuan proportions. Right now I'm just me. But pricklier.

After half a song of Madoka's pogo-stick dance moves and Ines's hardly-moving and staring seductively at Madoka, Bar Let's Go is a volcano of masturbatory impulses. A few brave souls venture onto the dance floor. Then a few more. A cheerfully violent pop anthem begins, and in seconds the black-and-white tiled floor is no longer visible. Horny boys with three beers in them shout along to the music, fists in the air. I'm ashamed to be human for a moment or two, until, as if on cue, the drug kicks in and I feel like giving everyone a big hug.

Madoka returns to the table red-cheeked and panting, Ines following behind her, a slight spring to her step that tells me she's high.

"Our work is done here," Ines says, saucer-eyed. She drags on a cigarette and points her chin to the door.

I make a stop at the ladies' room. Lean down and slurp water from the tap while I wait for a stall. On the toilet, I have a moment of bravery. Close my eyes and let the sound of Mom's voice roll over me with the drug.

Happened at some sports bar on The Danforth. He'd

stopped taking his drugs and—well you know how he is. Mags, he's asking for you. Sometimes he seems almost normal. Maybe those rednecks knocked something back into place. He keeps asking for you, Mags.

Save. Save. Save.

I can feel the gentle tug of the night as it starts to unspool. Serotonin floods my brain. Under my life's bedrock of crap and trauma, I can sense the gurgle and trickle of water. I'm so thirsty.

Tokyo at night, on drugs, is like being inside a pinball machine. Enough has been said about the neon. You can never say enough about the neon. The way it flashes and glitters for you like an electric ballet, the way you can ride the train at night, out of the city, into the suburbs, through town after town, and every time the train pulls into the station, without fail, just beyond the platform, the neon greets you—calls you into pachinko parlors, beseeches you to drink Sapporo beer, to buy Toshiba, to enjoy the delights of hostess clubs, stacked on top of one another like electric Lego. Stare at the neon and close your eyes. Open them and it's still there, imprinted.

Everyone on Omotosando-dori is beautiful, their skin seems to glow as if lit from underneath. Even the boys are pretty, pouty-mouthed, hair-do'd, dressed in the minimalist uniform of black and slate gray. You feel as if you've come to some understanding, but you're not sure what it is or how you got there. Something about the fragility of youth. It'll come to you. No rush.

Ines and Madoka are walking a few steps ahead of you, arms linked. Every now and again some joke is passed between them, and you can see their faces in profile, laughing, mouths open. You can't hear them above the hum of the street. They are miming bliss. You can see their teeth. Teeth never looked so lovely. At one point, at one joke, they lean in too far and knock foreheads. A moment of surprise, hands to heads. More laughter, which you can't hear.

You wish you could articulate the understanding that you've come to. You're dying to tell someone. Anyone. Any of the beauties walking past you would do. *I want to tell you something.*

Along the edge of the small creek behind Omotosando-dori, fortune tellers sit at folding tables, in the halo of light cast by paper lanterns. An old woman sells fried squid balls. Some teenagers practice an elaborately choreographed hip-hop dance routine.

At a bend in the creek, a small crowd has formed. Ines and Madoka insinuate themselves through the cooing little throng. You stand on your tippy-toes peering over the heads, but all you can see is an empty wire cage. On the inhale, a hand grabs you at the bicep, on the exhale you are standing next to Ines. You can see now that the cage is not empty. It's filled with fireflies. Hundreds of them, flickering on and off. The man opens the top of the cage, and the fireflies hover in a cloud of light above your heads. The cloud begins to splinter off, until you follow just one fly, squint as the light gets fainter, until you are staring into the dark and you remember to breathe again.

Even in your chemically altered state, your mind starts up the same old pattern. Take something good, pick it apart. Analyze it to death. Memorize it. Squeeze it dry until it's as special as the instructions on a shampoo bottle. Keep the fireflies in the cage until they drop one by one.

Ines turns to you. "How about Tengu?"

"I'm not hungry."

"Neither am I, but I want to look at food." She's shouting but it sounds like whisper to you. Like a purr. "Sit at the counter and watch the chefs."

Outside the pub, a wooden figure of Tengu, the mischievous little goblin with the six-inch nose, stands guard. Ines, who inexplicably knows every Japanese legend, informed you that the mythical figure of Tengu has special powers fueled by the water that resides in a bowl at the top of his head. Always wreaking havoc, Tengu could only be defeated if an opponent tricked him into bowing and spilling the water. For a moment, I think about hopping on top of Tengu's nose and simulating an obscene act, but I think better of it. I am above that. Besides, the last time I did it, a red-faced cop yelled at me for five minutes and I was barred from entering the restaurant. I was stoned and had the munchies. It seemed tragic.

I wonder why all of my good memories involve illegal substances.

"Remember when you fellated Tengu?" Ines asks.

"I did not," I say.

"Agedashi-dofu," says Madoka.

"—?"

"Fried tofu in broth," translates Ines.

"I love you all," I say.

"There's only two of us," Ines points out.

"I love you both."

Down the stairs, the cavernous pub is teeming with people, sitting elbow-to-elbow at the long communal tables, padding around the tatami floors in slippers. Squealing women sound like seagulls. The waiters scream at each other in rough boys' Japanese. The laughter is almost organic, rising in waves, pulling back into the clink of glasses, chopsticks against plates, and rising again, louder still. We lock up our shoes in little wooden cubbyholes and make our way to the counter seats, where we can watch the chefs. They shuffle around the narrow kitchen like an insect ballet, hands manipulating the food with a skill and intimacy that's almost sexual. Steam rises from cauldrons of soba broth. Skewers of chicken cartilage cackle over the grill. Not a bead of sweat soils the chefs' blue cotton headbands.

"I'd like to take them all home with me and have them suckle me like a mother pig," I say.

Ines nods. "Have them make breakfast."

"Can you imagine them all squished up around the hot plate in your room?"

"No, no darling. I know a love hotel with a gourmet kitchen room."

We go back to watching the cooks. Mention of the hotel veers my thoughts to Kazu. The high begins to ebb. My face melts into melancholy.

"You're not still thinking about what's-his-name are you?"

"Who? No."

"Why don't you just call him?"

"I don't have his number."

"I do. Got it from his cell phone while he was taking a pee."

"Why?"

"Because I'm crafty. Besides, you never know when knowing a guy like that will come in handy."

Tengu is underground. No cell phone reception. You feel like an anachronism. A person waiting to use a public phone. A salaryman screams into the mouthpiece. His suit looks tired. It wants to go home. The suit's man slams the phone down on the receiver. Slams it down again. Again. The swaying drunk girl in front of you sobers suddenly, straightens her spine, backs away from the phone. The man. His suit.

The screaming man comes to his senses. You've always liked the expression "come to your senses." You wonder where you come *from*. The man looks down at the receiver. His face softens in apology and he takes a step back. Bows at the phone. Shallow nods of his head leading into deep bends at the waist. You stifle a laugh. *A man bowing at a phone*. The man turns to the queue. Continues his frenzied apology. The people waiting seem to convey, with their smug pursed lips, that this is what one ought to do to make amends for a phone-booth hissy fit.

"I'm ashamed! I'm sorry! I'm ashamed!" the man barks in Japanese. He seems to shrink inside of his suit. Until he's all suit and scalp.

If it's greed that fuels the West, then shame must turn the karmic wheel in Japan.

You clutch the scrap of paper with Kazu's number. Clench your jaw. Squeeze your eyes shut and open again. Time curves in on you, and you're at the front of the line. It's your turn.

"Moshi-moshi," Kazu answers.

"It's me."

He trills a sentence of Japanese. Too fast for you to understand. Tacked on the end, a snippet of English.

Be patient.

Dial tone.

Along its edges, your field of vision is fractured, pixilated. You hadn't noticed it before. Now it is all you can see.

I'm sixteen. Frank is fucked.

Tony Varda holds my hand. When we walk, the carpet of dry leaves goes *shoop-shoop*. It's one of those Indian-summer days when you don't know what to wear. It feels like the whole world has been distilled down to two hands. One clammy. One trusting. There's a small stream, and he pulls me across. The wet sock will make a sucking sound with every step when I walk home, but I can't hear it yet.

At the clearing, there are two boys waiting. "What's going on?" I ask. (Like, as if she didn't know.) I giggle. I don't scream. (She fucking laughed, man.) Paul MacKay goes to hold my arms back, and panic squeezes the air from me. "No! I'll do it." (She wanted to put on a show for us.) The whole time I'm thinking about diving. "Keep your chin tucked in. Keep your legs together." I think I even mouth it, like a mantra. (She's fuckin' crazy, just like her brother.) I look down, past the white of my body, to the damp earth at my feet. I expect to see worms and those bugs that curl into balls, but there's already been a frost. Indian summer can't bring them back to life.

Frank is sitting on the front lawn when I get home. I sit down next to him. I've done the buttons on my shirt up wrong, and one side hangs down lower than the other.

"Frank?"

Frank rocks a little.

"Frank?" *It's the beginning of a new era.*

I smack him across the face. Frank hangs his head to one side, and I see Mom running from the kitchen, her mouth held tight, wiping her hands on her apron.

The staff at Air-Pro are stiffer, more robotic than normal. Their birdlike chorus of "welcome" trails off at the end when I step into the lobby. The five of them, pert and perfect in their faux stewardess uniforms, tuck their chins into their jaunty scarves and shuffle papers around in choreographed synchronicity.

The recruits huddled around the bulletin board disappear when they spot me, scattering in various directions like cockroaches after a light's been turned on. In the distance, I hear the click-clack-click of Ms. Nakamura's heels. I instinctively locate the fire exit. EMERGENCY TRAP DOOR reads the illuminated sign.

I turn down the hallway toward the bank of vending machines. A can of syrupy coffee is necessary before I can face Ms. Nakamura. Passing by the Deportment Studio, I catch a glimpse of a dozen or so recruits kitted out in black leotards and tights, lined up along a bar, like a rehearsal for *Anorexia: The Musical.*

The slogan on the drink machine urges me to "Enjoy Refresh Time." I doubt if I can comply. The clicking is getting louder, closer. For a moment, I consider hiding in the ladies' room, perching like a bird on the toilet seat until the coast is clear, but I don't, for the same reason I don't apply expensive eye creams—What's the point in delaying the inevitable? I put the coins in the machine, choose a can of black coffee, down it like a shooter, and walk toward the clicking.

I meet Ms. Nakamura in front of the Face Make Lab. Her mouth is a tight slash of red. In my heels, I'm a good five inches taller than she. Looking down at her gives me vertigo. To steady myself, I stare at the pulsing, bulbous vein near her temple.

She hands me an envelope. "Final pay," she barks. "Leave now."

"You're firing me?" I think about my work visa, which Air-Pro sponsors. "Why?"

The thump of blood at Nakamura's temple slows, relaxes. She must smell the fear on me. "You have tried to derange the recruits! Madoka-chan is telling!"

"We went dancing."

"Carousing!" she screams.

I can't help but laugh. It's either that or cry, and I'd sooner commit hara-kiri than shed a tear in front of Nakamura. I hold my hands up. "Okay. I caroused. I'm guilty." I do an exaggerated bow, nearly toppling over.

"Shameful!" She squints, purses her lips, scrunches her nose until her face resembles a crab-apple doll wearing lipstick. "You have face splotch and smell of meat! You are more worse than average foreign person."

"You are more worse than average vampire." I grab the envelope and head for the lobby.

On the way out, I corner Mikiko near the Emergency Trap Door. Her face is as poreless and unreal as always, but a faint crease appears between her eyebrows, which seems to convey sympathy. She grabs my elbow and holds it with the tips of her fingers, like a little knob. The gesture is inordinately intimate.

"Where's Madoka?" I ask her.

She clasps her hands under her chin and whispers, "Ms. Nakamura sent her for Intensive Remake."

"That sounds awful."

"*Iya, iya!* Madoka will be fixed!" Mikiko sighs wistfully, peers up at the fluorescent lighting panels on the ceiling.

"Fixed," I repeat. Like a TV set on the blink. Like a cat.

In the elevator, a lone recruit eyes me nervously. I have the urge to bark. Growl a little. Sniff my armpits to see if I really do smell of meat. When the doors open, I leap out, break into a run, zigzagging through the crowd, clipping shoulders. Briefcases swing from the hands of startled commuters, cars screech to a halt for me. I hit a clear stretch of sidewalk, feel the wind in my face, the sharp smell of exhaust fumes and ramen broth in my nose, lactic acid eating at my thighs. I hit a bottleneck, a queer forest of shiny heads, blue suits. A politician, wearing white gloves, stands

atop a van, screaming into a megaphone: "I have no religious affiliations! I am an honest man!" The blackboard
scratch of feedback vibrates in my ear.

If I had a clear path, I would run until I dropped, until
my legs or heart or lungs quit. I'd crumple to the ground
like a collapsible plastic camping cup. Flat. Spent. Too tired
to think. But I'm weak. The heat and crowds, the weight of
my body finally defeat me, and I slow to a dejected gait.

I turn down one of the narrow streets of Kabukicho.
Signs for massage parlors and karaoke rooms loom over me.
The streets smell of cooking oil, sweat, and exhaust fumes.
Like a factory that makes people. Assembles them, feeds
them, moves them. I feel like part of a machine. A faulty
part.

I walk for a good two hours, until my exposed skin feels
hot and tight from the sun. Winter has retreated suddenly
and briefly. A gaggle of schoolgirls revel in it—their white
shirts tied in knots above the bellybutton. Office ladies pro-
duce parasols out of nowhere, guarding their complexions
vehemently.

The heat starts to get to me. I crave a climate-controlled
labyrinth. I stop. Look for signs. I need the station. I find
an underground entrance. Lumber down the stairs,
through a dimly lit tunnel and into the station. Into the
enormous surge of bodies. There's a trick to navigating
through these crowds without bumping into people. You
fix your eyes above the heads of the people. Eschew eye
contact. Plot a course like a Zen monk doing walking med-
itation. Single-minded. Empty of connection. It works for

me for a good forty-five minutes. Chin up. Eyes dead straight. But eventually I need a smoke. Looking for a cigarette machine, I'm herded by a crowd surging from a bank of turnstiles. I see the glow of the machine over the crowns of heads. Drifting away from me like a stray helium balloon. I'm heading toward the exit. The glare of natural light comes as a blow. In a panic, like a dumbstruck animal, I turn back, but the crowd behind me prevents me from backtracking. It's straight ahead—to the street—or to the left—under a pedestrian walkway.

A sour smell gets stronger as I make my way under the walkway, duck under steel girders, and come to an open area. I look around at the tiny settlement in front of me. Dozens upon dozens of cardboard boxes fashioned into little homes—painted with swirls of color, surreal portraits, grim cityscapes. Smoke rises from fires set under tiny hibachi, the acrid smoke from kerosene heaters mingled with the smell of grilled fish. Little huddles of billy goat–bearded men sit crouched on their ankles, drinking sake and cans of beer.

I make my way along a walkway between two rows of cardboard homes. Peering in, now and again, at the tiny makeshift rooms. Some of them gussied up with curtains and photographs grayish-green with age. Music wafting out of others from cassette-tape players. The twang of the Koto, the click and roar of baseball broadcasts leading me along.

Out of habit, I clutch my purse tight, feel the hard lump of my disposable camera. Feeling touristy, I take it out.

Focus on a mural painted along a series of refrigerator boxes. A frightening cosmos of disembodied heads. Just as I'm about to hit the shutter, a tall, bony man flies out of the trap door hidden among the heads. Howls at me, lunges at me, wielding a stick. I start to back up and fall into the entrance of another box, waking up the tiny man curled inside. Throaty screams everywhere. I look frantically for the way back into the station. The man with the stick chases me back under the girders. Making my way through the knot of people streaming out the exits, I slip into the compartment of a revolving door. Breathe the stale station air like a fish plunked back into water. When I turn around, a Japanese guy is standing there. "They don't like to have photos taken like things in a zoo."

He's taller than most Japanese men, brushing six feet, with tanned skin and heavy-lidded eyes. His T-shirt reads AMERICAN USED FREAK.

"Thanks for the advice," I say.

American Used Freak stares at me for a minute. My heart rate makes its way back to normal.

"Do you live in Japan?" American Used Freak asks.

"Live," I say. "In a manner of speaking. Yes."

I look up at an electronic sign. It tells me it's thirty-two degrees Celsius. It tells me to drink something called Pocari Sweat.

I gulp on the thick air. There's something weird about American Used Freak's eyes. Something cold. Something that doesn't add up. He's too old to be a student. But he doesn't look like a salaryman. His hair is too long. The details are all slightly off. The loose jeans and sneakers. The Rolex watch and stiff posture.

I realize I'm still clutching the envelope from Ms. Nakamura. The paper is dissolving with my perspiration. I can see the scowl of some prime minister on the ten-thousand yen notes. Worst-case scenario: I could be on the missing-girl adverts. The missing girl could be dead. I imagine a garbage-bag sarcophagus. Somewhere hidden, damp. Where it's quiet. Worst-case scenario: Kazu will never call me again.

I look at American Used Freak. He hasn't shifted his gaze. Worst-case scenario—he could be a psychopath. My little voice says, *Who gives a shit.* "Do you want to go to a love hotel with me?" I ask.

'm seventeen. Mom was right. I've found my niche. I'm the school slut. My venture into the social realm is over. I watch a lot of documentary television, smoke until my fingers turn yellow, and barf up my food for kicks. Whispers follow me like Pigpen's swirls of dirt. At school, my favorite place is with my head stuck in my locker. The slams and rummaging in the adjacent lockers reverberate like thunder and lightning in my ears. It's all I can hear. I learn to love the smell of rotten fruit and leaky ballpoint pens. I have no face. No swollen eyes. I'm not really here.

One day, I'm walking home from school. I cut through the University of Toronto. There's a place by one of those ancient old buildings. The ones obscene with stonework and stained glass. There's a place, under a fire escape, look-

ing out at a field carpeted with dirty snow and dead grass.
I like to get stoned there.

I'm crouched down smoking one day, when I see Mom.
She's walking with her shoulders up by her ears, bracing
herself from the wind racing between the buildings. The
woman with her has no hat on. She has that haughty
Germanic beauty. Her shoulders are relaxed. She has short,
spiky hair, so fine and blond it looks like feathers. She puts
her arm around Mom's shoulder, leans into her. I close my
eyes before they kiss.

The joint hisses when I crush it out on the ground. I
think about genes. A high school pariah who just might be
a schizo dyke. Beautiful.

We rent motel rooms after the prom. It's an old honey-
moon motel from the fifties. Someone tells me the tubs are
heart-shaped. We have to pay a damage deposit. The rooms
smell like Lysol and something feral.

"You're not still sore about that thing in the woods are
you?" Tony asks.

"What thing?"

"We were kids," he says. "You know?"

There's a yellow water stain on the ceiling. Someone
who left the bathtub running. Someone who didn't get
their damage deposit back. It looks like a Rorschach test.
Siamese twins joined at the shoulder. We were kids. Yes.
What are we now? I wonder.

He grabs me and pulls me down onto the bed. "Fuck, I

want you so bad." We're on our sides, his hand grasping my hipbone like a handle. Our noses are almost touching. I can smell his breath. I think of Eskimos. "You're killing me," he says. For a minute I let myself imagine reaching over for the lamp on the bedside table and splitting his head open with it. I can feel his cock pressed against my thigh. I don't feel excited. Or scared. I feel the tug of the inevitable.

After it's done, the knocking starts. "Stop hogging the room Ton!" someone yells. I sit up on the edge of the bed and look at the table lamp. See that it's screwed into place on the synthetic woodgrain of the nightstand. I go into the bathroom and run the water while I pee. A short hush, then cheers. The slap of high fives. The water comes out brown, then yellow, then white. The tub is tub-shaped. I'm disappointed.

When I go out, someone hands me a can of Canadian. Each time the door opens, a gust of air blows in. Someone yells, "Shut the fucking door!" It's the kind of night between winter and spring, when the air feels like a tonic. I want to throw the windows open. Luxuriate in the last sting of the cold.

Alone is not about people at all.

After graduation, I get a job at a bagel shop. We have twenty different kinds of bagels and twelve different toppings. I'm snotty to the customers, but my boss doesn't care. Something about the way I ignore him leads him to believe I'll eventually sleep with him.

I want to get my own place, but I can't seem to save

money. It's all I can do to keep myself in weed and diet Pepsi. Mom and I are at each other's throats.

Dinner conversations go something like this:

"What's this?"

"Weanies and beanies," Mom says chirpily.

"Fuck, Mom. This isn't dinner!"

"Maggie."

"It's prison slop."

"You used to like weanies—"

"Yeah, so did you," I mumble. Then louder, "It's starch and lard. Where're the veggies? The greens?"

"They're tofu weanies and beans in a tomatoey sauce. Now eat up!"

"This is shit!"

"You're welcome to cook for yourself."

"Oh go lick pussy, Mom."

She picks up our plates. "Lovely, Margaret." Dumps them in the sink. "Lovely." Beans slip like lava down the drain.

Frank eats alone in his room.

take the train with American Used Freak. He buys his ticket from the machine. Doesn't offer to pay for mine. The carriage is nearly empty, but he stands up. Holding on to a hanging strap with both hands. Swaying with the jerk and pull of the train. We don't talk.

When I was ten, I watched the neighbor's dog pull a hedgehog through a chain-link fence and tear it apart. I imagine, as we make our way, in awkward silence, from Shibuya station to Love Hotel Hill, that sex with American Used Freak will sound something like that. Desperate and hungry. Plenty of slobbering and groans.

I lead him to the same hotel Kazu took me. Choose the Marquis de Sade Room. It has fancy pink furniture, a four-poster bed splayed with various ropes, gags and cat-o'-nine-tails. At the last moment, before pushing the button on the illuminated panel, I check my mobile phone to see if Kazu has called. *Be patient. Be patient.* I could go home and sit in my room. Listen to the cockroaches scuttle behind the walls and worry about money and visas and my sanity. I could. I look over at American Used Freak, who hasn't said a word since we left the station, who looks strangely stoic and handsome in the kind, muted light of the private lobby. I push the button.

When I come out from the shower and drop my robe, American Used Freak makes a sound, the kind of sound you'd make as you take a last suck of air before jumping from a high place into deep water. There's a moment of hesitation, some sweat that collects like dew above his lip.

I walk over to him, stand close, so that my nipples harden against his T-shirt. "So, American Used Freak." I put a finger to his chin. "What's your name?"

It takes a few seconds, but a smile creeps onto his face. A crooked grin. He grabs my finger and brings my hand down to my side. "You can call me Used," he says. "No need for formality."

I toss him a coil of rope, push aside the cuffs, the riding crop, the whips and blindfold, and curl up on the bed. In the fetal position. Somewhere between seduction and submission. Used skillfully binds me to the ornate headboard, puts a finger to his temple in contemplation, then proceeds to stretch my legs, spread-eagle, to the bedposts. As soon as I'm bound, after Used tugs at the knots to test their strength, when I'm sure I can't wriggle my way out, a sense of calm blankets me. There's no use struggling. I go completely limp. My body begins to feel like a rubbery, lifeless thing. I have the feeling that something is being drawn from my belly, through my skin, through the dirty mattress, the smoky carpet, through the ground, to the center of the Earth. I turn my eyes and find myself in a mirror, relieved that I'm still here. Still solid.

Used doesn't touch me. He doesn't even take his clothes off. With a languid nonchalance, he makes his way around the room. Dims the lights. Switches the music off. Buys a beer from the vending fridge, pulls a chair up to the end of the bed, and lights a smoke. In the dark room, with the shadows playing on his face, Used looks like a different person. Older. Less chirpy and benign. Fear squeezes my heart. I'm getting wet.

Time passes. Three cigarettes. I'm dying for a puff, but I don't ask.

"You like this," he says.

I stay silent for a moment, wondering if he wants an answer. Something in the way he holds his head, chin lifted slightly, a long ash hanging precariously from the cigarette poised before his mouth, tells me he's expectant.

"I like to be passive," I say. "Do you know what that means?"

He takes a deep drag on his cigarette. "I am good at English. You needn't grade your language." The words tumble out with his exhale. "Passive. To obey without argument. I don't like passive."

I want to explain to him. Maybe being passive is allowing the other part of yourself to take the lead. But I stay quiet. Scan the room. It is windowless, but on one wall there is an illuminated panel framed with velvet curtains, to give the impression of a window. Used stands up and walks to the side of the bed, brushes aside a hair that's caught in my eyelashes. His hand hovers around my face for a few seconds. I can smell the sharp odor of nicotine, but my craving for a smoke has gone. He smiles. Grabs hold of the pillow and pulls it from under my head, drops it to the floor, and returns to his chair.

"I like these places. Love hotels." He gives the room a once-over. Nods. "Do you know the words in Japanese *omote-ura?*"

I shake my head.

"*Omote* is the front. How can I explain? The mask. In the love hotel there is no *omote.*"

Used stands at the foot of the bed, cigarette hanging from the side of his mouth, and unties my legs. "These things are difficult for gaijin to understand." The knots seem intricate, but he releases them as you would the laces on your shoes.

"It's not rocket science," I say. Trying out my voice.

"No, but it's subtle. Something Western people don't appreciate."

I try to think of something clever. "*Wabi-sabi,*" I say.

"Ha! Love hotels do not have *wabi-sabi.* Simplicity and elegance. No."

"What's your point then?"

"I am returnee—I was educated in America. So I will never belong in Japan. Truly. But I am certainly not one of you. Lapping at freedom like a dog at his bowl. No appreciation."

He moves to my head. In the moment it takes him to untie my hands, I glance over to the mirror. Without the pillow to prop up my head, I can only see a sliver of myself. The ash from his cigarette falls on my neck. "So sorry," he monotones, and roughly flips me onto my belly.

"*Ura* is what lies behind." He collects my hands and feet and holds them together in a little bouquet, twists the cord around, ankles to wrists until I'm hog-tied. Steps back for inspection, mumbles a little in Japanese *(Dou shiouka? What shall I do?)* and wedges the pillow under my hips. "*Ura* is the true thing."

My neck and back are starting to ache.

"Are you uncomfortable?" Used asks.

I shift a little bit. Open my knees a bit wider.

"If you move the next position will eventually hurt, and the next one. You ought to get used to how it is now."

Used is quiet for a moment. I can't see much—some bedsheets, a patch of wall, the sliver of me in the mirror. My sense of hearing gets sharper, as though I've been scanning radio frequencies, going through the crackle and hiss and finally turning the knob just so. I hear the room—the hotel—perfectly. The sound of Used smoking. The suck and the long exhale. I hear, through the wall, the sounds of a couple doing it. The creak of the bed. The rhythmic *ah-ah-ah* of the girl.

Used is at the side of the bed. His hand on the inside of my thigh. I want to change the energy in the room. I lift my hips an inch, let out a little moan of anticipation. "See how wet I am?"

"I could kill you and no one in Japan would care. Only about bad press maybe."

"That's not true," I mumble into the pillow. "Someone would care."

Used takes his hand from me and moves away. "Just wait," he says. I hear the hiss of a beer can opening. "I'm going to tell you something."

Used's Something

"When I was a high school student," Used tells me, "I knew a girl. There was always gossip about this girl, maybe because she was quiet and beautiful. Very white, with small lips. Probably because she had no mother. She lived alone with her father. No one knew about her mother. Perhaps she died, or ran away with a lover. I don't know. The girl had an odd name as well—Lily—like the flower."

"I thought at the time that Lily and I were perfect for each other. My father's company had sent him to England for six years. I had gone to school there. I was what they call 'returnee.' My Japanese-ness was less than others' maybe. And I could speak English. Anyway, I was good at sports and taller than the other boys, so I got some respect that way. Still, I was different. Like Lily."

Used and Lily would meet in the afternoons at her

apartment, when her father was still at the company. She had a small, Western-style bed and her room was filled with all sorts of girl things. Posters of singers, dolls and toys, stacks of comic books. In the absence of a mother, Lily kept the small apartment clean for her father, but her bedroom was a mess. The floor was carpeted with clothes, every surface was cluttered with makeup, the window and vanity mirror were a collage of tiny Print Club machine photos. It almost hurt your eyes it was so full of things, but Used liked being there. She'd make a snack and some tea, and they would talk a bit. Then she'd crawl under the covers of her bed, pull the duvet up to her chin and look at Used.

As soon as he took his school-uniform jacket off and found room next to Lily on the small bed, his cock would get hard and his face would flush. This seemed to do something to Lily, push some trigger, as if arousal began in another person, and only after she saw it would it move to her body. Taking care not to let the duvet fall below her collarbone, Lily would shimmy out of her clothes and press herself against Used. She would never let him remove his clothes and she would never, under any circumstances, let him see her body.

They never had sex, but in the sincerest, sweetest meaning of the term, they made love. Used felt as though he wanted Lily to pass through his skin, to be absorbed into him.

Used assumed that after a few weeks, Lily would lose her shyness and he'd be allowed to see her body, but it never happened. If anything, she became more and more vigilant about keeping the covers pulled up to her chin at all times. He wondered if maybe there was a scar or a burn on her body—some mark she was too embarrassed to show him. Under the duvet, after they'd made love, he would run his hand over her thighs and back, along her abdomen. The skin seemed uniform and unflawed. A little trail of fine hairs led his hands down from Lily's navel to the tuft of hair on the gentle rise of her pubic bone. He observed her body without eyes—charted it—and Lily would moan a little or fall into a light sleep.

"One day Lily's father returned home early. I was in her bed when we heard the scratch of the key in the lock. He coughed loudly—that awful salaryman cough from too much smoking. He yelled, '*Tadaima!*' and Lily put her clothes on in panic. It all happened so fast, and I was so frightened, I didn't even look at her body as she dressed. She was going to go into the living room when she turned around and searched through some clothes piled on the floor for a cotton cooking apron. The kind housewives wear, with stupid English slogans and teddy bears. Her apron said: I FEEL COOKIES. She looked scared. Her hair was fuzzy and knotted at the back. After that I always loved these stupid English sayings on things."

Used stayed there in Lily's bed until her father went to take a bath. Lily kissed him good-bye and laughed a little in relief as he left.

Things went on like this for a couple of months—the talking, the tea and snacks, the sweet, shy lovemaking— until suddenly Lily told Used that she couldn't see him in the afternoons for a while. She had to take care of her grandmother, who was ill.

"I tried to make myself busy after that. I played baseball with my school friends. Once or twice in the month after that, Lily asked me to come over, but things were changed. She seemed tired most days, and I was too full of wanting her to act as normal."

Just after winter began, Used started to hear gossip about Lily. She was seeing some boy from another school. She'd go to love hotels with him and bring him to her apartment.

Used started following Lily after school. He would enter the subway carriage next to hers, stand by the through-doors, and watch her. She was tall for a schoolgirl and always wore a red muffler, so it was easy to find her among the tangle of commuters. After a week of following her, Used started to learn Lily's body language intimately, as though it was his own. The way she'd rock on her heels when she was waiting on the train platform. Chew at her fingers when she was nervous. Nod her head again and again when her friends babbled at her, like she was urging them on, or urging them to finish. There were things about her that he did not know. Like how she evaded him some-times, in the narrow streets around the station, disappear-ing for an hour or two then turning up again at the ticket kiosk. Like what she was thinking when she was alone.

"I waited by her building one day. She didn't arrive home until after eight o'clock. All the time that I was waiting there, looking up at the balconies of her building, I remember feeling deeply sad. Almost every balcony had some similar arrangement of the same objects. Some potted plants. A clothesline. A futon draped over the rail to air. I looked from building to building and almost each apartment was identical. Then I started to think about the people in every apartment. I wondered how many of them felt this awful pain of mine.

"For just a moment I felt comforted by the thought that I wasn't alone, but that didn't last long. The sadness, the jealousy, the comfort, they turned into a hard piece of anger. If I squinted my eyes, the buildings looked like grids. If I looked at Tokyo from above, the city would also look like a grid of little squares. I was simply something to fit in one of the slots. The lonely schoolboy. The unsatisfied. I sat there, on the cold cement of the entranceway, and when Lily finally walked up, I didn't feel anything else, just anger."

Lily invited him in but told him he couldn't stay long.

"My father will be home in an hour or so."

Lily fussed over the tea in the kitchen. She burned herself on the handle of the teapot and sucked her finger.

"How is your grandmother?" Used asked. A blank white space was filling his body, like anesthesia taking hold.

"She's okay," Lily took careful little steps with the tray in her hand. "Are you hungry?"

"Why don't we go into your bedroom, huh?"

"Well, my father will be coming—"

Used took the tray from her and put it on the table.

Maybe she could feel the white space inside him, or maybe she felt guilty, but her hand was stiff and clammy when he led her into the bedroom.

She was still wearing her school uniform—the scratchy brown tunic and blue cotton blouse. He pulled the tunic off easily, holding her hands above her head. She didn't struggle. The buttons on the blouse were trickier, and he thought for a moment about just ripping it open, letting the buttons pop off. His mind worked strangely. He thought he ought to be patient, since she'd be the one—in the absence of a mother—that would have to sew them back on.

Finally, he had the shirt off and her bra—the kind that unsnaps in the front—splayed out like little white limbs at her side. She wasn't wearing panties. Used went to toss the crumpled tunic off the bed when he saw that Lily's panties were balled up in the pocket.

"I'm sorry," Lily said.

"I grabbed one of the scarves that she had draped over the posts of her bed, and tied her hands together to the top of the bed. Lily whimpered a bit, like a cat. I stood back to check once if she had some sort of scar or burn or something. Something to explain her shyness. Then I tied each ankle to the posts. She had no scars. I left her there."

At the station, the train pulled in and spit out a flaccid load of salarymen. Used wondered if Lily's father was among them. A jolt of panic charged up through him. He thought for a moment about running back to the block of apartment buildings. Untying Lily. He pictured himself. Running. Gulping wind in his throat. But the picture dissolved, and all he could see was the sudden expansion of the field of possibility. Like a drawer filled with options had opened, and he knew he'd be rummaging through it from then on.

The room is hot. The air stale, twice-breathed. These rooms aren't meant for talking. There's a click, and the TV comes on. Loud. The syrupy chirp of an advertising jingle. My legs, bent up like chicken wings, pulse with pain. It starts in my knees, crawls up to my hips, down to my ankles, the arch of my feet. It comes as a relief when finally there is no part of me that is comfortable, no good to hold up to the bad. I can sense some movement, a shift in the distribution of the muddy air. I look at my patch of wall. Breathe into the coverlet that smells of chemicals and peaches. The mattress heaves and I can feel Used behind me.

"Used," I wish I knew his real name. I can feel him behind me now. He must be on his knees. "Are you okay?" His hand is hovering over my back. I can feel the heat coming off him. "Say something."

He traces a line down my back with his index finger. His hands are dry. My back dewy with sweat. He presses his palm on the sole of my foot, hooks his thumb and forefinger around my ankle as if measuring me. He takes the half-blue, half-blond hairs that are pasted to my face and tucks them behind my ear. In one swift movement, he unties me. In the time it takes me to straighten my legs, the door clicks shut and he's gone.

Everything in the bathroom says discreet. But it's spelled wrong. The soap, the shampoo, the toothbrushes, condoms, hand lotion, razors—everything says "Diskrete." The name of the hotel. I run the bath and turn to the alibi radio station—the constant sound of trains for the comfort of the cheating husband when he calls home. The pitch and roll, the hollow voices of the announcers in the background, the whoosh of the doors opening—it's perfect bath music. The Diskrete bubble bath has no telltale scent. Nothing has a scent. It's as though I'm not really here at all.

I'm eighteen. Frank's twenty.
He hangs around the house all day. Mom has to remind
him to take a shower. He's prone to crying fits, so Mom
says things like "You smell a little ripe, dear," or "A good
hot shower will make you feel like a new man."

Most nights, Frank sits on the front lawn, cross-legged,
clutching a spiral notebook and a pen, watching the traffic
lights intently.

Mom stands in the kitchen, parts the curtains, and peeks
out at him.

"What's he doing?" she asks.

"Fuck if I know."

"Language, Margaret."

"I think he's losing it."

"Don't say that!" She sits down at the table, pulls the ashtray over, and lights a DuMaurier. "He's just oversensitive." Mom's lost weight. She's up at six every morning, jogging for an hour. I see her sometimes, running full-speed, right up to the driveway, the cords of her neck stretched taut, skin shuddering over her cheeks. Her body has become like a greyhound's, skin shrink-wrapped to muscle, the thick muscles of her neck supporting her head like an oversized pedestal. I tell her I'm proud of her, but I secretly miss the flying squirrel's wings of fat under her arms. I miss normal.

Mom's sent Frank on an errand. Milk. Toilet paper. Cigarettes. I go into Frank's room. The curtains are closed, and the room smells like neglected damp towels. I find his spiral notebook and open it. Page after page of the words "green," "yellow," "red," columns and columns of it, *greenyellowred*, *greenyellowred*, *greenyellowred*, in a jittery, childlike scrawl.

I turn to leave, and Frank is there. Arms like dead things at his side. Expressionless. I'm not sure when he grew so tall, when his small impishness stretched out into the skinny, ashen-faced, greasy-haired man in the doorway. I'm afraid of him.

He walks past me, to the television, pops in a video, and sits down on the bed. It's a nature video, a monkey sitting in the elbow of a tree, chewing at a mango pit.

"Frank?" I say. He doesn't look at me. I walk toward the door.

"Watch the monkey scare the children," he says suddenly. I turn, look at the screen, but it's just the monkey, the tree, the mango pit. I wait for the children, but they don't appear.

"Watch the monkey scare the children," he says again. Blue light flickers over his face.

The exit of the hotel leads to a shady alleyway. I look up to a honeycomb of balconies and air conditioners. Then to the side—to the black car idling there. Some dust rains down on me from a shuttered window, and I look up to see a hotel attendant beating a futon. The sight of a human being startles me, then consoles me. But as swiftly as safety washes over me with the dust, the arms disappear inside the room, the futon is yanked back in. Sun reflects off the black of the tinted windshield in a star of light. I walk toward the street, and the black car follows. The air stops in my throat.

I pick up my pace. There will be people on the street. I'll be safe. *I could kill you, and no one in Japan would care.* I'll be safe.

The car is beside me. The door opens, scraping against

the wall, blocking my way. A man's arm. Shoulder. Neck. *Someone would care.* "Come in the car," Kazu says.

I plant my hands on my hips and let the air spill out of me. Hot and bitter. "You scared me."

He frowns. "Are you safety girl now?" His eyes open just to slits. "I don't think so." He points at the passenger seat, and I climb in.

"Don't you want to know why I was at the hotel?" I ask.

"I am not a stupid man," he says, placing his hands on the steering wheel, precisely at three and nine. "And you are not a patient girl."

"I'm sorry," I say feebly.

Kazu starts to drive. Winding down tiny back streets. Clinking his rings against the steering wheel.

"I said I'm sorry."

Kazu pulls out onto the street. "Only a word. I'm sorry."

"How did you find me? Were you following me?" We pull onto the expressway, and Kazu's driving becomes more aggressive.

"This hotel." He swings his arm back as though Hotel Diskrete was directly behind us. The expansiveness of the gesture disturbs me. I look back. The gray outgrowth of the city seems to be trailing away with the waning day. "This hotel is *my* hotel. I am owner. Do you understand?"

His hotel. The implications roll over me like a cold sweat. Was he watching us? What is the exact distance between anger and violence? Where am I right now?

"I have your boyfriend," Kazu says.

"Have him?"

We drive for another fifteen minutes or so. Past a sad-looking amusement park. The Ferris wheel spinning uselessly without passengers. He slows and pulls into a private parking lot. *"Asoko,"* he says. *Over there.* We stop. "Get out."

The parking lot overlooks the water. In the distance, joggers as tiny as ants make their way along the water's edge. The parking lot is empty except for a lurid pink van with big wheels and a neon underbelly.

"He's not my boyfriend," I say. "I've never had a boyfriend."

"Nani?"

"I mean I've had lovers. I've had regular fucks. But no one has ever called me their girlfriend. Except maybe this weird stalker guy. But he was deluded—"

"Stop talking," Kazu says.

Kazu opens the trunk and reaches his arm in, helping American Used Freak out as a gentleman would help a lady from a carriage. Used's hands are tied together in front of him. His palms pressed together as if in prayer. His nose is broken. A mess of pulp and bone and red. It hurts to look at him. But I can't turn my head. One perfect bubble of blood on his nose inflates and deflates as he breathes. He looks at me glassy-eyed, then something comes into his eyes, a brief clarity—*This is all your fault*—I read from the short glimmer.

Kazu turns. Presses his palms to his temples. "I am not a bad man," he says. It looks like more words are trying to come out. Twisting in his mouth. He swallows, and they're gone. He reaches in the trunk and pulls out a black wooden box, closes the door, and places the box down.

"This knife," he says. "Sushi knife." Kazu picks up the ancient-looking thing. Inspects the blade close to his face. "Maybe two million yen," he tells us. "Gift, *ne*?"

"Kazu—" I choke his name out.

"This knife for cutting big things. Head *to ka*, spinal *to ka*—Maybe so sharp—" he presses his finger against the blade, and slowly blood sprouts in a perfect line across his fingertip. "No feeling."

"Kazu—" This is the way it will go. I am the chorus. *Kazu, Kazu*—

"Behind the face every man is bad." He brings the knife down Used's front. The knife grazes his chest, slicing a window in the T-shirt, his chest is tan, unscathed. The knife stops under his crotch. Kazu turns the knife to face up. I try to close my eyes, but can't. With a flick, the tip of the knife slices through the cords around Used's wrists. For a moment, Used just stands there. Perfectly still. The rope falls away. Kazu makes some gesture. A quiet word in Japanese. Then Used runs. Jelly-limbed. Flailing. Toward the water's edge.

Kazu packs up the knife. Cracks his neck and packs the box away in the trunk.

All I can think of is Used riding the Ferris wheel. Hoarding freedom.

"Get in the car," Kazu says.

A shouting match in my head. *He's a fucking psychopath. He really loves me. He's a fucking psychopath. Oh, God, he really loves me.* "Where are you taking me?"

"To a safe place." His eyes disappear behind sunglasses. "For talking."

Kazu is silent as we drive. I try to calm myself by looking at the scenery. Industrial wasteland melting into housing estates melting into neon-tangled entertainment districts. And back again. Every so often, along the highway, a life-sized cardboard cutout of a police officer stands in admonition. We hit a bottleneck of traffic and idle beside one of the cutouts. The cardboard cop holds his mouth tight, eyes squinty and vigilant. Warning me of something, but I don't know what.

The air is hot and stagnant in the car. Like sitting in a dog's mouth. "Can you turn on the air-con?"

"No need," Kazu clips. "One minute. Arrival."

I look out at the tangle of wires crisscrossing over the maze of residential streets and lanes. Laundry draped everywhere. Abandoned bicycles and children's toys lying in piles, like modern art. Tokyo is back there somewhere. We pull out onto a main street, into a parking lot. *"Hai!"* Kazu says. "Shin-Yokohama Ramen Museum. We are here."

"Where?"

"Ramen museum," he says. "History of noodles." He jerks his head, urging me out of the car. "Also safe talking place," he adds.

We make our way through the huge concrete structure to the *Shitamachi*—a detailed replica of a Tokyo street circa 1950—old wooden structures housing ramen and sweet shops. Tour groups and families crawling through it at a snail pace, cameras clicking like a thousand disapproving mothers' tongues.

"*Onaka ga peko-peko,*" Kazu says. "Starvation, *ne?*"

Kazu chooses a shop, and I find myself playing the woman—I shoo him to sit down while I wait at the counter with the other wives and mothers. I look back at him, sitting at one of the rustic tables, palm toward me, examining his fingernails. I want to serve him. I feel repulsed with myself. But it feels good. I can't hide my stupid smile as I walk back to him.

"Do you know your walk is interesting?" he says.

"It was you following me, wasn't it?"

He waves his palm left and right. "No need to follow."

"My walk?"

"*So desu ne.* Like a Japanese child. Five years maybe. Before *giri* begins. Duty."

"Duty," I say, linking my arm with his and leading him to the row of wooden facades near the exit. A small group of teenage boys and beleaguered fathers crowd around a chrome ashtray, sucking joylessly on cigarettes.

"You are loose legs, free legs. I have my job. My wife. I have made promises."

We find an empty bench. Kazu says, "Excuse me," and drags the ashtray and its pedestal over to the bench. The smokers look stunned for a moment. Kazu says, *"Dozo! Dozo—"* And the little group shuffles over with the ashtray, nodding their heads in thanks.

"Listen to me, Margaret." He puts his ramen bowl on the side table.

"I thought you were starving?"

"My wife has suspicion."

"So? All wives do. That's part of the job."

"My wife is a dangerous woman. Honestly speaking I am afraid of my wife. I'm sorry." He bows his head at me and I feel like I'm clawing at the edge of a crevasse. Ice falling away on me. "I believe she knows your face. Maybe she followed you."

"Why don't you come with me—to Bali or somewhere."

He shakes his head. "Impossible."

"Why?" I whine.

"I told you. Please listen. I have duty."

"Fuck duty."

"You are *wagamama* girl."

I know this word. *Wagamama.* It means, "spoiled." "Willful." I start to cry.

"I'm sorry," Kazu says. He wipes away a tear with his knuckles.

"Only words," I shoot back.

"I am a businessman. *Itsumo*, good for business, bad for business. *Kokoro* has no meaning. The heart, *ne*?"

"So?"

"So, so, so. I looked down at her in the bed with the finger in mouth and I loved her."

"Thumb."

"Thumb. I love you. Thumb. Okay."

Kazu's phone rings, and he holds up a finger. Walks away from me. I look around at all the families. Deeply immersed in their steaming bowls. Content in the fake city.

Kazu's ramen goes cold. I look over at him. He seems to be having a heated conversation. I pose for a photo with two teenage girls. We hold our hands out in the peace sign and say *cheese-u!*

Kazu comes back and grabs me by the elbow. "The dishes," I say. Japan has made me polite.

"Leave them," he barks.

He pulls me toward the back exit. Stops at a long corridor. "Please listen," he says, handing me an envelope. "Take this and leave Tokyo."

"No."

"Yes. It's dangerous. She knows."

"We could be happy—I have a feeling."

"Happy is important to you."

"Of course it is—"

"In Japan harmony is important."

"Kazu—"

"Don't go back to your room," he tells me. "And do not call me on the telephone again."

He turns and leaves me there. Fingernails scraping hopelessly at the edge. The pocket of ice calling me in.

Harmony. I imagine Kazu, his wife, and me singing together. Shoulder to shoulder. Singing and smiling and swaying. I don't have to open the envelope to know it's filled with a pile of money. I wander toward the station. To Jiro's, in lieu of a home.

I'm nineteen. Frank's been diagnosed. It's Thanksgiving, and I'm afraid of getting fat again. Frank sits in the living room, staring blankly at the television, rolling imaginary beads between his fingers and thumb.

"Frank! Come and help me with the gravy."

Frank repeats, "Gravy."

I sit at the kitchen table, chewing celery sticks into spikes and harpooning pimento stuffed olives with them. Strings of celery stick in my teeth. The waist of my jeans digs into my belly. I don't want to be here. I want a drink.

Frank's face is puffy, freckled with acne over his nose, on his chin. He looks like an old man. Like an old zombie. Tall and crooked and slow. I watch him stir the flour and water. He stirs like a watched person. He does everything like a watched person.

"Can I have a beer?" I ask.

"It's early," Mom says, pulling back the quilting of her oven mitt and making a show of checking the time. "Oh, go ahead. Make me a gin and tonic, will you? Do you know how?"

"Uh, gin and—" I snap my fingers, grimace. "Tonic?"

"Smart-ass."

Frank repeats, "Smart-ass." He begins to laugh but ends up shuddering.

I hand the drink to Mom and whisper, "Is he Rainman?"

Frank turns and screams, "WHO'S PEEPING?"

With her oven-mitted hand, Mom pats his back, shoots me a look. "Shhhh," she says.

The beer makes me want a cigarette. I wonder what the cigarette will make me want.

In the bathroom, hidden behind the toilet, I find a balled-up tissue filled with half-dissolved pills.

Mom confronts Frank at dinner. "Are you taking your pills?"

Frank's face twitches a little. "Yes."

"The pills help you so I want you to take them —swallow them, okay?"

Frank jerks his head to the side. Smiles.

"Frank?"

"Mmm-hm."

"Okay, let's eat."

What are those Buddhists on about, I think. *Stay in the moment.* Fuck the moment. I want to go back or forward—

any way but here, now. But I can't go back—back to family dinners, begging Mom for a sip of her wine, teasing each other, telling stories, eating so much I have to undo the top button on my jeans. Can't go forward—can't meet Frank halfway, in some shadowy place where the world is like a reflection in a fun-house mirror, where the nuts and bolts of life disappear into a trippy dreamscape. A place like that must be better than this.

"Who's the smallest woman in the world, Frank?"

No answer.

"Frank, what's the world record for breath-holding?" I think I see something behind his stare, a fragment. But it vanishes.

Meet him halfway. "Green, yellow, red! Green, yellow—"

Mom slams her fork down on the table. "Stop it, Margaret!"

"Fuck, Frank! Say something!" I grab his hand—it's cold and sweaty—but he pulls it away, jumps out of his chair. Lets out a wretched bleat.

"Margaret!" Mom screams.

I see a warped reflection of Frank in the shiny black of the refrigerator door, his arm held over his head, the glint of the blade. That's when I start running.

Don't go back to the house," Ines tells me as I sit down.

"Seems to be the consensus."

Jiro pours me some beer. He has a white hand-towel wrapped around his head, like a bandanna. He's in his usual blue work clothes that look like a karate uniform. I loll my head around a bit. I'm still stiff. Jiro narrows his eyes. "Hard day's night, *ne*?" He says this every night.

"Weird day's night, *deshiou*?" I cackle. Glug down my beer. One of my neck stretches draws my eyes to the wobbly table in the corner. It's stacked with shoes and handbags. A knapsack hemorrhaging clothes leans against the wall. Ines sighs. "Police showed up at the house today."

For whom? I'm thinking. "For what?" I say.

"I didn't stay long enough to find out. Let's just say my

165

papers aren't in order." She points to a tiny run in her stocking. "I crawled out the window."

"With all that shit?" I ask.

She glares at me. Nostrils flared. "A lot of cock-sucking went into getting that *shit*."

"Kazu dumped me because his wife found out."

"Don't fight a Japanese wife," Ines says. "You'll lose."

"I could take her." I flex a bicep. Quickly pull my arm down again at the pathetic sight of it. Ping-pong ball on a noodle.

Ines sighs. "Let me tell you something about Japan. People think it's run by men but that's a myth. The women are in charge. Mothers. Wives. They control the money. Tough guy Kazu probably gets an allowance from his wife like all men in Japan do. The women fuel the economy with their shopping. Impeccable taste—most of them anyway. Luxury all the way. They stay behind the scenes because they're smart. The men die from overwork and the women do the decorating. They've got it all figured out."

"But I love him," I say. Embarrassed by myself.

Nobody says anything for a few minutes. Jiro stands at a distance, hands clasped in front of him, lost in the melancholic love ballad on the radio. Ines, with her elbow on the bar, swirls the beer in her glass, inspects it as though it were fine wine. "I'll go tan my tits in Bali." She starts forcefully applying lipstick. "Change is good."

"I can't stop thinking about him. It's like a rash. I mean, I fuck guys all the time. I can't explain why he is different."

"Fish have no word for water," Ines says and downs her beer in one gulp.

"*Ashita ga aru*," the men on the radio harmonize. *There is tomorrow.* It's an infectious tune. The kind that makes you want to sway along.

"Fuck tomorrow," Ines says. She has the look of someone who's had the blood drained out of her. Pale and defeated.

"How old are you?" I ask her without thinking.

Perhaps because the question comes out of nowhere, sneaks up on her, she answers quickly. "Thirty-four," she tells me.

I'd always imagined her as younger. Twenty-six. Twenty-seven. But as soon as she says her age, I see the extra years on her face. In the brackets around her mouth, the slightly crepey skin under her eyes.

As though she is reading my mind, she puts her hands on her face and holds the skin back until she's all cheekbones and slanted eyes. "Do you remember when you were about eighteen—what you imagined thirty-four to be like?"

"Like—adulthood."

"Like death." She drops her hands, and her face slips back into precarious youth.

"But you're the sexiest thing ever," I tell her.

"True," she smooths her hair down. "But still."

The gap between songs on the radio is long and poignant. Jiro holds up our empty bottle of beer. "Drinking time?" he asks.

Of course.

Ines becomes serious suddenly. "I need to ask you a favor, darling. A big one."

"Okay."

"Give me your passport. Let me get out of the country, then report it stolen."

"But we look nothing alike."

"We all look alike," she says, averting her eyes. Sucking on her cigarette.

"Sure," I say. "My passport is your passport."

Ines squeezes my bicep. The look on her face terrifies me. *You are a force of nature*, I want to say. "This is probably our last night together in Japan," I say.

"Cause for celebration, gorgeous. What shall it be?"

"More beer?" I suggest.

"More everything."

Through the yellowing frosted glass of the sliding doors, I see the outline of Adam. Tall—taller than the doorframe, spindly and ungraceful. Ines slinks off her barstool and locks the door.

"Come on!" Adam calls. "I've got a surprise for you birds."

Ines looks at me. "What do you think?"

"Well, he does have a surprise."

"Is the surprise a liquid?" Ines asks.

"No."

"Chemical?"

Adam bangs on the door.

Ines presses her cheek against the glass. "If I open the door a slit, can you slip the surprise in sideways?"

"No, no, no. Fucking hell. It's *cultural*." He says "cultural" like a child sounding out an unfamiliar word.

Ines flips the lock open. "I've got to see this." Adam slides the door open and enters with his nose in the air, decked out in a black suit and minister's collar, fanning himself with a handful of tickets.

"Japanese thee-ah-tuh my friends."

Ines grabs the tickets. Inspects them. Squinty-eyed. "Good God." She hands the tickets to me. "They're Kabuki tickets. At the fucking National Theater."

"A small gift from the father of the bride to me—the holy man—to you. The skanky boozehounds. Enjoy. Enjoy."

Ines plunks down on her stool and scowls. "Nice timing, Adam. I'm leaving tomorrow."

"Leaving where?"

"Here. Japan. Have to get out before I'm deported."

Adam turns to me. "And you?"

"I'll stick around for a bit. Still got a good couple weeks before Air-Pro cancels my visa sponsorship." I take a gulp of beer, sit up straight and proud. "I got canned for deranging the students."

Ines shakes my hand. "Good work, Marge."

"The state of you two! Couple of ne'er-do-wells."

"Come boozing with us?" I ask Adam.

"Can I wear the collar?"

"Might have some trouble scoring," Ines says.

I look across the bar. "And you Jiro? Come out with us?"

Jiro crunches his eyebrows together. "Eight years already I'm open. Every day. 7-11 *ne*?" He starts to wipe the bar. We watch him. Watch the lines of his face shift. He stops, and I notice for the first time the faint line on his ring finger. The soft skin where a ring was worn for years. I'd like it if all of our past showed as marks on our bodies. On the bus you could read your neighbor instead of the newspaper. A history in scar tissue.

Jiro drops the rag. Lifts his chin. "*Hai!* Let's enjoy together." He grabs a bottle of wine from the high shelf. Then two more. "Only one life each person."

We all follow Jiro. Each of us in our own reverie. Walking in a little clump for what seems like an eternity. When we turn onto the street that cuts through Yoyogi Park, I ask Jiro where we're headed.

"My favorite Tokyo place. Spirit of Tokyo."

When we reach the middle of the huge green space, he leads us up a pedestrian walkway, down into the park. Stops on the steps and sits down. "Sit! Please!" From his bag, he recovers a bottle of wine, four tumblers, and a bag of wasabi peas and dehydrated squid strips.

I look around. "This is it?" I ask. The spirit of Tokyo?

Adam crunches his nose. "Smells like piss, mate."

Jiro pats his hand at us. From somewhere in his belongings, he shakes out a thin blanket and spreads it out at the top of the stairs. Sets up a little picnic.

Just as we're about to clink cheers, the music starts. The soulful whine of a saxophone radiating from under the concrete stairs. Jiro takes a swig of wine. "Practice space," he says. "Japanese apartment very small, *ne?*" Jiro lies back and points at the sky. A sheet of black strewn with stars. Tokyo is so alive with its own lights, I've never seen the night sky like this.

I think of the Sunshine Building and the panorama of Tokyo. Yoyogi Park sits near the center—just over to the west a bit. The sprawl of the city radiating around us. So many people. Lives. Below us, Jiro's blanket, with a vague smell reminiscent of ciggies and incense. Wine spills gone to vinegar. And above us the stars.

The saxophone is melancholic. Sensual. Like a tranquilizer, it eases me onto a corner of the blanket, the low notes pressing on me like bags of sand, the high notes like fingers raking my scalp.

Jiro points at the three-quarter moon. "Lunatic," he says.

Adam holds his glass out, "Just a few more months in Nippon and I will be."

"Rabbit," Jiro says. "Lunatic rabbit."

"Lay off the vino, Jiro my man."

Ines lays back on her elbow. "No, you pleb. He's talking about the rabbit on the moon. We see a man, Japanese see a rabbit. It's an old folk tale. A monk on a pilgrimage comes to a clearing in the forest and asks the animals for help. All the critters find food and shelter for him but the rabbit has nothing, so he throws himself on the fire as a meal for the monk. The monk carries the limp little bunny body up to the moon."

"Morbid," I say.

"Life," Ines tells me.

I want a happy ending. It must happen sometimes. Why not to me?

Quiet comes over us. Even Adam looks contemplative. Jiro hums a little to the music. He makes smoking look like a religious experience. When the wine is gone and the saxophonist packs up, we all look a little lost. Some clouds appear out of nowhere and obscure the moon. *Kill the music. Kill the lights.* Ines says, "I need to dance." And we reassemble, pack up our picnic and depart the spirit for the flesh.

I don't fight it. It just seems right to go to Bar Let's Go. A gesture of sanity. Seeing things for what they are. This is what I do in Japan. Drink cheap booze and listen to the same ten songs over and over.

We find a table on the mezzanine. A lookout. I dig in my purse for a lighter and pull out Kazu's envelope. Take a peek inside and realize the notes are all *ichiman-en*. There must be at least ten thousand dollars. "Drinks are on me," I say.

There's some commotion near the door. A pale worm of a gaijin being restrained by two meathead bouncers. A pack of onlookers collects to feed. I turn back to the bar. Order a bottle of champagne. Some whoops and hollers form the dance floor. Some more from the doorway. Can't see for the crowd.

I look up at the mezzanine. At our empty table. The energy in the room has suddenly shifted. The crowd seems thin. Concentrated around the edges of the room. The exits and the restrooms. The champagne is plunked down in front of me. Ines grabs me by the shoulder. "Come on. The cops are here."

"Wait," I hold up the champagne bottle. "Let's drink it in the loo."

"They're checking alien identification cards. Someone was attacked in the subway by a foreigner," Ines says. "They've got Adam. His tourist visa is expired." She points her chin at the door. Cops with flashlights are scrutinizing the contents of a blond girl's purse. She stands slumped into one hip. Head held at an angle. The gathered clubbers look like a mangy pack of dogs.

Ines pulls me behind the bar. "*Gomenasai*," she says, cutting a path through the startled bartenders with her tits. The bottle of champagne held overhead like a trophy. We find the swinging door into the kitchen and enter the tiny hot pit of chaos. The back door is propped open in hope of a breeze. We make for it. Sigh in relief and breathe in the decay and piss of the alleyway. I grab the champagne from Ines and pop the cork." "Fuck, I never paid for this," I laugh. Catch the cascade of bubbles with my mouth. A waiter appears at the kitchen door, waving a bill. A cop yells, "Stop!" The bottle shatters at our feet.

For two drunk girls, Ines and I run pretty fast. After a couple of blocks, I look back and watch the cop—he can't be more than five-feet-two, pumping his legs like a little robot. Blowing his whistle frantically. The look on his face—pure determination, bordering on lust—tells me he's actually going to catch us. Then the wind carries a fetid smell over. "This way," I scream at Ines, and dart down a back street near Shinjuku Station.

Once in the thick of the cardboard box city, which at this hour is darkened and quiet, we huddle between two boxes like kids playing hide-and-seek. The policeman's whistle pierces the air, somewhere nearby. It feels like my heart will jump through my ribs. Curtains are parted on one of the boxes, and a brown, withered hand calls us in. I duck my head in the box. Ines pulls her heels off and slinks in. Inside is like a Morroccan tea house. Box leading to box. Rugs and cushions strewn everywhere. The gauzy-bearded homeowner crouches like a bird by the curtained front door. He looks like something made of leather. Tough skin stretched over delicate limbs. He gives us a suspicious look. Then gestures roughly for us to relax.

A cat is curled in the corner. It lifts its head up. Gives us a piss-off meow. By the doorway, I see an old pair of leather construction-worker shoes. Laid out carefully. Like artifacts. The man serves us gritty tea. Studies us.

"Nice place," I say.

Ines translates.

"Good tea," I say.

"Will you quit it?" Ines asks.

The little man seems to get the gist of it and hacks out a laugh.

We sit.

I think about harmony. About the cardboard box men. Itinerant workers outside the bonds of family, company, community. Cast into poverty after the bubble burst. Cast adrift. Permanently off-key.

I think about Frank. And me. Ines. Cast adrift.

I bury my head in my hands. Heels of my hands pressing into my eyes. "Shit. Shit. Shit."

"Shhhh," Ines says.

Sounds outside die. No sign of the little cop and his whistle. Ines looks at me. "Okay. Let's think darling. Where should we go? We have to be discreet."

Discreet.

"I know the place."

On the way out, I take a few notes from the envelope and slip them under the construction shoes. I nod thank-you. The man's expression doesn't change. He's the symbol of something, but I don't know what.

We get the Merry-Go-Round Room at Hotel Diskrete. I crawl up onto the bed and pull off the coverlet. Slip myself into the envelope of the stiffly starched sheets. Animals in lurid pastels encircle me. How can this be sexy? For a few minutes, I try to work out how we will avoid the cops tomorrow. And Kazu's crazy wife. Tokyo suddenly seems tiny.

Ines comes out of the bathroom, patting her hair with a towel and smirking.

"What is it?"

"I was just thinking," she says, sitting down on the edge of the bed. "I could write a love hotel guidebook." She drapes the towel over a unicorn and lets her robe fall to her waist. She pats her shoulders. "Do you mind, darling?"

"Lost girls and love hotels," I say, extricating myself from the bedclothes. "The definitive guide." I sit Japanese-style, legs bent under me, rub the freckly crest of Ines's shoulders. Exhaustion starts to settle into my body. A creeping fog. *Chapter One. The Versatility of The Love Hotel. What most people don't realize is that apart from the obvious sexual function, the love hotel can provide a refuge for the lost girl. A place to regroup. A place, festooned with the miscellany of childhood, to contemplate all the wrong turns, the bad choices, the fuckups.* "Have you ever thought of going home?" I ask.

"Home," Ines says, moaning a little. "Last time I went home I lasted three weeks."

"Three weeks isn't bad."

Ines lifts her hair into a twist, exposing her neck. "All the people I knew—they were just quoting *Seinfeld*." She drops her chin to her chest. "Everything felt like a stupid in-joke." I knead the stiff shank of her neck. "And I felt—*out*." On the TV, three girls in bikinis compete in a hard-boiled-egg-peeling race. "That's good," Ines purrs.

"I should go to Italy and meet some swarthy olive farmer."

"An idea."

"With piercing eyes." I lie back on the bed and stare up at the mirrored ceiling, like a lovestruck teenager, like a whore on a coffee break. "And a drafty stone villa at the edge of an olive grove."

"Big equipment." Ines curls in next to me, tits cupping my arm. "A thick cock beats love any day." She throws her arm across me. I think of cats curling together for warmth. We lie there. The poignancy of our silence is grating.

"Love is an oasis of horror in a desert of boredom," I finally say, putting on a game-show announcer's voice.

"Good God."

"I read it on a napkin at a café in Tokyo Station."

Ines's hand moves over the little bump of my stomach, to the waistband of my panties. Slips inside, raking the tuft of thick hair. I observe it happening like a film. As if on cue, my hips buck a little. I look down at the two of us. I feel like a plank, lying on my back next to the S of Ines's body. At the end of the bed, a pink-and-blue pony eyes me disapprovingly. I reach down for Ines's hand. "Ines. Come on."

"Come on what?"

"I don't have the right equipment for you."

"I'm an equal opportunity slut," Ines says. "Boys, girls. I'm not fussy really." She pulls her hand away roughly. The waistband of my panties snaps at me. Ines lies back and fumbles at the bedside for her smokes. Her hand hits a button, and the merry-go-round starts to turn, accompanied by a high-pitched version of "It's a Small World After All."

"I used to think if I traveled around enough I'd eventually find the place where all the people like me are," Ines says. On the TV, the girl with the yellow bikini and the orange tan peels her egg the fastest. Ines turns away from me and curls into the fetal position. "Now I don't think there's such a place."

"But there are people like you—I mean there's me, for instance."

"Sure. But we never really stay together in one place. We're all just orbiting each other." It sounds like someone's moving the furniture around in the room above us. I start to get the bedspins. I remember there's something you're supposed to do to stop the bedspins. But I can't recall what it is.

Ines begins to snore. The most delicate snore imaginable. Like a baby's chortle and snort. The rhythmic quality of it starts to make me drowsy, and I pull the sheet up to my chin, tuck it in around Ines. Slip my thumb in my mouth. Slip into sleep.

I dream about the missing girl. She sits at the foot of the bed, smoking the last of my butts. Smirking at me. She looks whole but she's not really. When she moves to position a pillow between the small of her back and the pink unicorn, I can see that she's constructed loosely in parts—like a marionette.

"Are you dead?" I ask her.

"Do I look dead?"

"Are you following me?"

"Why are you running?"

Her voice is exactly as I'd imagined it—sensuous, with a teenage girl's nasal insolence at the edges.

"So what now?" she says.

"Bali maybe."

"Then?"

"India or China—I don't know. Fuck. Maybe I'll just go crazy."

"You've been in the anteroom to crazy for ages now."

I fumble around for a smoke, but the pack is empty. The dead girl smoked my last one.

"It's about time," she says.

"How the fuck—" I look back at her, but she's not there. It's Frank. Knife in one hand. "It's time," he says.

I wake up sweaty. The windowless room won't betray the time, but something about the air tells me it's early. Ines is gone. Bags and shoes and all. I sit up and grab for my purse. No passport. I flip through my wallet. Take out the envelope of cash and the Kabuki tickets. I split the cash into two piles. Stand up and inspect the room. It looks, to my nearly sober eyes, like a child's bedroom. Except for the bowl of condoms on the headboard, it's all kitsch and innocence. Running my hands over the haunches of the unicorn, I find an opening where its belly meets the silver pole and I squeeze the rest of my identification, my phone and one pile of yen into the hollow innards of the beast. Stand there for a moment, without an identity.

In the bathroom, I nearly slip on Ines's hair. Silky ropes of it carpet the tiny space between the tub and the sink. In an act of solidarity, I grab one of the pink Diskrete razors and hack away at my own mop. After ten minutes or so, I inspect myself in the mirror. Tufts of hair sticking out everywhere. Somewhere between Jean Seberg and a mental patient.

I send the money down the vacuum chute to pay, and

leave the Merry-Go-Round Room. *Change is good*, I tell myself. It's a busy day at Hotel Diskrete. Most of the rooms are taken. I close my eyes and lean against the panel. Wait for a beep. For contact. I don't know where I'm going. I just follow the lights on the floor. Obediently.

In the Hawaii Sunset Room, a projector plays a looping film of a beach at sunset on the wall opposite the bed. I sit there, slotting wasabi peas into my mouth and memorizing the progression of colors. Blue to purple. Red. Orange. Gray. Black. Someone's scrawled their initials on the wall, spoiling the effect. Finally I pick up the phone. I pause before dialing Kazu's number. Pause between each digit. It seems to ring forever. And then the voice mail. "Meet me in front of the National Theater at three P.M.," I say. "Please."

stand in the center of the square in front of the theater. It's a Japanophile's wet dream. Ladies in kimonos shuffle along, parasols perched on their shoulders. Ginkgo trees line the square, behind them cherry trees, still green and dormant. Sometimes in Japan everything seems to fit together. Four perfect seasons leading you through the gamut of emotion. The dead cold of winter—the damp of depression—broken when it seems unbearable by the bacchanal of cherry blossom season. Everything interlocks perfectly.

An hour passes. People fill the square, then disappear into the theater. I stand there like a human sundial. He's late.

A recipe: one part desperation, one part panic, a teaspoon of lust, and a pinch of hope. It leads me, after another hour, into the theater. Just in case he's waiting there. Why the fuck would he be waiting there? Maybe he got the message wrong. It's more romantic. Waiting in the theater. I'll pick him out from the back of his head. Slip into the seat next to him. Put my hand in his lap.

The theater is dark. I look for a bald head among the audience. Row by row, I study the heads. On the stage, a man wets his finger and pokes a peephole into a paper shoji screen. Watches a lover's rendezvous. Body poised in concentration. I wonder how much can he see through the tunnel vision of the peephole. How much he must construct himself to complete the picture.

An usher taps me on the shoulder and I turn back, away from the strange light of the theater, past the bowing usherettes at the door, into the city again.

I've always loved dusk—the feeling of the day receding— night crawling in to conceal everything. A chance to hide. To lick one's wounds. But tonight, something in the sky cracking gray and purple, something in the closeness of the air—it makes me walk faster. I don't know where I'm going.

Near Harajuku Station, I watch the Goth lolita kids in their costume-like black dresses with crinolines, stripy Pippi Longstocking socks, sunken smoky eyes on baby faces. They stand in little groups, posing stiffly for photos by tourists. On the fringe of the scene, some boys dressed as spacemen drag on cigarettes and eat crepes stuffed with whipped cream and strawberries. For a moment I feel serene—a freak among freaks. But I keep walking.

I walk up the stairs to a pedestrian overpass and pause in

the middle. Look over Yoyogi Park, the tori gates of Meiji Shrine. I've started to know the city well. Too well. If I stay here too long, a time will come when I cannot get lost—when each of the thousands of unnamed streets is like a familiar walk I could do with my eyes closed. The idea chills me, and I continue along the overpass and down again toward Shibuya. If I can't get lost, at least I can be swallowed up by a crowd.

Eventually, I find myself at the giant five-pronged intersection at Shibuya Station. On the overhead video screens, pop starlets compete for the pedestrian audience. I look across at the statue of Hachiko— the dog who waited for his deceased owner for ten years outside the station. Hundreds of people stand around the doggie. Craning necks and clutching phones. Waiting for someone.

The light turns green, and the mass of people begins to move. Through the forest of heads, I keep my eyes on Hachiko. I'll wait there. For ten years, if I have to. Maybe they'll erect a statue of me. People will know me only by my first name. I'll be a landmark. An urban myth. A place to rest for a smoke.

I get bumped by a thin woman— she looks straight at me—her face like a bug in giant Chanel shades. She makes some gesture, and I look down at her hand. The sushi knife. I stop in front of her. *Don't fight a Japanese wife.* I lose my breath and fold over for a moment. A schoolgirl next to me shrieks. Something's wrong. *So sharp you don't even feel it.* The crowd parts. I fall to my knees, blood pooling around me, reflecting the neon.

PART THREE

Remember Your Heartful Life

The woman in the tiara says, "My name is Watanabe. Please call me Audrey." She pushes something at my mouth. Wipes my face. I hear moans and howls in the background. The squeak of wheels. *I've gone to hell.* The woman in the tiara leans closer. Gurgles something. My eyes scan her. *People in hell wear name tags.*

My eyes start to focus, the Vaseliney film clears, and I see that the tiara is, in fact, an old-fashioned stiff nurse's hat. I reach for my side—feel the lump of bandages under my flimsy gown. My mind flashes back.

"Frank," I say.

"Audrey," she says.

"No. Frank—my brother—he—" I try to sit up, but the pain in my side makes moving impossible.

She points to her nose, intones in sweet condescension, "Ah-do-rhee. Nurse."

My brain is floating in drugs. "My brother stabbed me."

"Brah-zah? No." She pushes me back down firmly by both shoulders. "Don't overdo it. Now is relax time!"

Audrey starts to pull the curtain around the bed, and I push myself up on my elbows. Pain twists my innards. "Tell me what happened."

She yanks at the curtain, and before it's closed, sticks her head back in. Moon face and dingy vinyl. "It was the wife," she whispers.

Audrey tells me, "Tomoko is really vixen woman. Her efforts cause of when Yukari did suicide. Hidetoshi is the handsome detective. Ex-boyfriend before of Tomoko's twin sister, Hitomi, who is also good nurse like me." I slip between a drugged stupor and a waking state punctuated with pain and force-feedings. Audrey tells me what's going on in the Japanese soap operas. It's comforting somehow— all of the double-crossings and evil twins, miscarriages and family secrets. It makes me feel normal.

It is like Frank is in the room with me. The two of us. Beaten down and bloody. He's a young Frank. Twelve or thirteen. Long-limbed. Nervously happy. Grasping hungrily at the world.

Audrey comes in, and I'm crying.

"Why sad?" she demands.

"I'm not sad," I tell her.

"What are you?" she fiddles with my IV bag. "Pain?"

"I'm nostalgic."

"What is it? Bad?"

"I don't know how to describe it Audrey. Forget it."

"Important to know words. Meaning. History. I'll find the history for you. Information is key. I know from English school."

"Fine," I say with a laugh.

By the third day, they've eased off the sleeping pills, and I'm awake for most of the day. The food is strange—strangely delicious. It comes in paper bags stamped Takashimaya Department Store. Pretty chi-chi for a hospital.

Audrey insists on spooning an elaborate jellied orange dessert into my mouth. She wipes my mouth and sits down to torturously read the *Japan Times* to me.

"Why is the food here so good?"

"Japan has—" She holds a finger up and goes to her idiom dictionary, "extensive life expectancy." Snaps it shut. "Fault of food."

"No—the hospital—why does the hospital have such good food?"

"*Iya iya.* You are funny. Families are bringing the food. There is no hospital food. Only kiosk."

"But I have no family in Japan—"

"*So desu ne.* Fat man bringing your dinner. Giant fat man. *Chotto kowai.* Scary."

"I'm confused."

"Your body is sick," she tells me slowly. "As well your head. Listen to me practice English."

I settle back in the bed. Gaze up at the inside of my eyelids.

"Listen! *Cherry Blossoms in Bloom in Fukuoka!*"

191

I open one eye a slit to look at Audrey. Her eyes are sparkly, and she hops a little in her chair. I close my eyes. Inside of my eyelids is black with red snow.

"Do you understand?" Audrey asks. "*Sakura!* Cherry blossom! Beautiful times are coming! Open your eyes!"

"Heavy teaching load perverts teachers," Audrey says haltingly. *Hebi road.* She begins to read the article to me. The words poke at me.

"Just the headlines," I tell her.

She frowns. "*Hai!*" Her pronunciation becomes deliberately worse. "Just-*o*. Head-*o*-rines. Okay Julia."

In the hospital, they do not call me Jane Doe. They call me The Gaijin. Audrey thinks of a new name for me each day. Katherine. Betty. Mariah. Finally, I tell her, "My name is Margaret."

She looks at me disapprovingly. I've exposed myself. My charade of amnesia. Audrey pulls her shoulders back. "If that is your choice. *Shimashiou.* Let's call you Margaret." She turns back to the paper. "Typhoon in Okinawa. Pop Star's Mother Speaks Out. Missing Girl's Remains Found."

"Stop."

"May I read?"

"Read it. Please."

Audrey snaps the paper and holds it close to her face. Sounding out the difficult phrases. Slow-motion punches. *Dismembered. Positive identification.* It seems like forever, but she finishes the article.

I turn my head away. Pull the sheets up around my shoulders. Stare at the curtain. I wish I had a window.

Audrey shuffles over to the other side of the bed. "Don't be sad, Margaret-chan." Pats my forehead gently. "Remember your heartful life."

When they tell me I can leave the hospital, I get a room at a business hotel tucked in behind the glare of a suburban entertainment district. The sound of the pachinko parlors—the frenzied electronic music, the piercing chime of the machines—becomes like white noise: when it stops, I can't sleep. I just lie there and listen to the banter of the staff as they spill out into the alley. Calling out to one another. *"O tsukaresama deshita!" You must be a very exhausted person!* Yes, I whimper. I am.

The scar is shaping up well. Soon the wound will heal over. Turn into a raised red worm along my midriff. I run my hand along it. Imagine the stories I'll tell. An emergency appendectomy in a dirty backwater hospital. A religious fanatic with a broken wine bottle. Or maybe I'll just stay quiet, enigmatic, brood in silence about lost love.

The police ask me if I can remember my name yet. If I

can remember anything at all. I lie to them. *No, nothing at all*. They ask me if I like Japanese food. *I think so, yes*. But the stabbing is never mentioned. They tell me I must stay in Tokyo. The foreigner liaison officer, a humorlessly efficient middle-aged man, clutches his briefcase over his crotch and tells me, "In your personal belongings there was found a large sum of Japanese yen. We police will hold this money until that time when your identity is determined." "May I have an allowance please?" I ask him. His face goes red. He reluctantly places his briefcase on the floor and hands me an envelope with both hands. "A receipt and twenty thousand yen for your daily needs." I can't get out of the country on twenty thousand yen. They know that.

When I walk in, Jiro squeals like a girl. "Marge-san! So happy. Please sit. *Onegaishimasu*." Using a chopstick, he pops the top off a beer bottle, pours some into two squat glasses. We clink cheers, and Jiro says, "Adam-chan in jail."

"Jail?"

Jiro searches his pockets and takes out a piece of paper. Hands it to me.

Dear Jiro,
I'm stuck at the Kansai Immigration Detention Center.
Bloody Japs (no offense, mate) will let me go as soon as I
come up with the money for a plane ticket. Start a collec-
tion for me, will you? The food here is shite.
Adam

• • •

Jiro produces a teapot from under the bar. Shakes it like a piggie bank. "Already six thousand yen. Adam-chan has many lover-girls."

I laugh. "How about Ines? Have you seen her?"

"Ah!" He produces an envelope from under the bar. Smacks it down in front of me excitedly. Before I can look, he says, "Inside your passport."

I open up the envelope and pull out the passport. Tucked in like a bookmark is a faded business card. Shanti Lodge. Ubud, Bali. "Tasty food. Good swimming. Clean sleepings."

"Ines," Jiro says, tapping his forehead. "Smart girl. Never worry."

Clean sleepings.

"Yes," I say.

In the space between two sips of beer, I make my plan.

I stand in front of Hotel Diskrete, my tiny bag of belongings slung over my shoulder, looking at the windowless exterior for half an hour before I make my way to the lobby. Once inside, I pause again. Wait for the sensation of being watched. Wait for it like a lonely girl waits for the phone to ring. But it never comes, so I pad over to the room console. The Outer Space Room is taken—the light behind the photo of the space pod bed darkened. I find the Merry-Go-Round and push the button. Follow the trail of lights on the floor.

Once I am inside, a wave of fear and loneliness rolls over me like nausea. I fumble with the vending fridge, flop down on the bed, and slurp from a can of beer. I put my feet up on the unicorn, feel around his belly with my toes. "You have something for me?" I ask. He stares at me with a tight smile. I down the rest of the beer and crawl over to the beast, reach my hand up and feel around. The documents and money are still there, in a little hollow near his neck. I breathe. Turn on the mobile phone to listen to Frank. But the message is gone. It takes me a moment to register. It's gone. I give the unicorn a pat on the nose and lie down Think about sleep. It seems like, another planet.

When the alarm clock flashes four A.M. and my TV choices are reduced to lounge singers and porn, I wedge a shoe in the door and venture out into the hallway. Every now and then, I hear a squeal or a moan from one of the rooms. The elevators won't take me anywhere. But I stand in one anyway. Going nowhere. I'm left to make a semicircle around the first floor. I start speaking out loud. *Meet me in Kyoto. Meet me in Kyoto.* On my third lap, a tiny man in a threadbare gray suit appears out of what looks like a broom closet. He tiptoes toward me, stops at a distance, and in a stage whisper calls, "Gaijin-san! Go back! Now is sleeping time." I stand there for a moment. The little man nods at me and shoos me away with a nervous smile. I head back to the room. Sleeping time.

The bullet train robs me of the sensation of speed. It glides over the continuously welded track so smoothly it doesn't feel like we're moving at all. I buy two cans of beer from the refreshment trolley even though it's seven in the morning—maybe because it's seven in the morning. There's an old woman sitting next to me. She must be a hundred. Shriveled lemon for a head. Collection of bones under a fan-print dress. Jaunty pink sun hat sitting in her lap. If I were her mother, I'd tell her not to stare. She's fixated on me like a child at the zoo.

I give her the bug eyes. She sniffs at me. Puts her sun hat in the seat pocket. Pulls out a fancy bento box. The kind with vegetables cut into delicate flowers. The kind with ingredients I can't identify. Seaweedy, flowery, undersea-creaturey things.

I feel the need to be genteel. Take the beer can away from

my face and pour some into the plastic cup. I find my pinky finger rising in the air as I sip. Some deeply recessive prissy gene popping up. The old lady gives me a smile when I tuck the digit under the other fingers. She reaches in her straw bag. Brings out another pair of chopsticks and hands them to me. "*Hai! Dozo—*" *Go ahead,* she tells me. I poke at a wiggly white-and-pink thing in the bento box. Pop it in my mouth and nod thank-you. Pass the cup of beer to her. Color comes to her face. She takes a nice gulp. I eat more seaweedy stuff.

After we polish off the second can of beer. After Michiko-san shows me a photo of her dead husband. A photo of her dead mother. Her dead brother. A photo of her standing next to Placido Domingo. After she joins me in the smoking car for a ciggie and green tea from her thermos. And tells me she had an *omiae*—an arranged marriage. That she never had a lover. That she thinks African-American men are handsome. Especially Denzel Washington. After all of that, I sleep deeply. Slumped against the window. I sleep until Michiko nudges me. "*Fuji-san! Fuji-san!*" I open my eyes as we pass the perfect symmetry of Mount Fuji. Symbol of Japan. Clouds hanging in reverence around its peak.

Kyoto Station is not a dark archipelago. There's no hiding here. It's all soaring ceilings, glass, and light.

While her grandchildren look on in shock, Michiko and I hug good-bye on the platform. For an old thing, she has a good grip on her. I imagine my stitches popping open. My innards spilling out onto the platform. Troops of upcountry Japanese forever thinking this is what foreigners do at train stations. Spill their guts.

. . .

I find a dilapidated old guesthouse. Sleep in a long tata-mi- mat room with four other women. A group of middle-aged Australian women who buy beer from the vending machine and sit in the kitchen late into the night talking about temples and camera shops. Their twangy animated voices soothe me. I can't tell them apart, with their weath-ered tan faces and bodies like potatoes with toothpick legs. They share also an earthy goodness. "You look like you've been through the wars," one of the ladies says to me. I get drunk with them and tell them a short version of my story. It is disjointed and messy. "I need to write it down," I say. They hand me another can of beer and tell me I need to get pissed.

"You're a brave one," one of them says.

I say no. "I'm just good at running." It's in my genes.

A month before I left for Japan, I was in the food court of the Eaton Centre in Toronto. And I saw my father. He looked pretty much the same. A bit jowlier. A little less Bryl cream in his hair. He had two kids in tow. Girls about six and ten. And a blond woman with thin legs in white jeans. They seemed in a rush. The woman holding her mobile phone between her ear and shoulder and rushing on ahead. My father leaning down on one knee and wiping the corner of the younger girl's mouth. The girl grimacing. The blond woman turning around and barking something. The four of them disappearing down an escalator. The whole thing took thirty seconds, but I sat there with my paper plate of shrimp fried rice in front of me for a good hour. Thinking happy thoughts. Of something sharp to cut away memory. A rewind button. A clean slate.

"You can start over," I say to no one in particular.

After one night, the ladies take off for Mount Fuji and I'm left alone in the huge room. I pull my futon out of the closet and roll it out next to the window. The panes of frosted glass are cracked and mended with sealing tape gone yellow with age. The whole wooden structure creaks and shudders when someone walks in another room, a reminder that I'm not alone. In the morning, I can hear birds. A breeze blows the branches of a cherry tree against the window. A light rapping telling me to get up. The kitchen is littered with empty beer cans. But I feel sober.

I'm sitting in a suicide-inspiring waiting room at Kansai Immigration Detention Center. A few animated Filipino women seem to be conducting three conversations among themselves and another three on mobile phones. Everything in the room—the curtains, the calendar on the wall, the magazines—looks like it's been left out in the sun too long. Washed out and brittle. I imagine all the multitudes of people passing through this room. What's happened to them, happened to me—all the waiting, all the endless disquiet—it's made us like energy vampires. Sucking the life out of the room.

I look up, and Adam's standing there. His hair hangs

down in a mop in his face. His clothes are looser. He makes a show of putting on a pair of sunglasses. He reminds me of the drummer from *The Muppet Show*.

He takes the glasses off again. Looks serious for a moment. "Fucking hell. What happened to you?"

I'm not sure if he's talking about my hair, my scrawny frame, or the expression on my face. It's one of those times when you have so much to say you can't say anything at all. I kind of pucker my lips up and shrug. The tears come fast. When Adam leans over to give me an awkward hug, I jerk and shudder into him.

"Hey, hey. We're going to Bali. You should be chuffed."

"I'm not going to Bali," I tell him.

"Why not? Leave me alone with Ines? She might get me into trouble."

"I'm going home." *Home.* I suck in air. Five liters or so in one huge sniff. "I have a brother there."

They tell me you can get all types of good-luck charms at temples in Kyoto. That you can buy fortunes. If your fortune is bad, you simply tie the strip of paper to a tree and buy another. That you can grope along a dark labyrinth to a chamber lit from above, where the Buddha's belly lies. You can touch it. A blessing. That everything will be clear.

I walk up the narrow street leading to the temple grounds. I'm wearing the jeans I was stabbed in. The hospital washed them clean somehow. In the pocket, I find a small note card. In Nurse Audrey's careful cursive: *Dear Margaret. I want to be your long lost friend for always. Audrey.* And then in block letters: NOSTALGIA. FROM THE GREEK WORDS *NOSTOS* FOR HOME AND *ALGOS* FOR PAIN. A BITTERSWEET LONGING FOR THE PAST. In parenthesis, (Margaret-chan, we Japanese say *natsukashii*.)

The pain of home.

Everything will be clear.

I believe it.

It's morning, and the hordes of tourists haven't arrived. Mist shrouds the temples. The quiet is slithery. I open a map. Trace with my finger the route to the Buddha's belly.

When I look up again, they are there. The children. An army of them. Kitted out in their blue-and-white uniforms, yellow caps, stiff leather book bags strapped to their backs. They wear shorts. Soft little legs. White socks. The bobbing mass of yellow hats moves toward me. Behind them, I glimpse a beleaguered teacher, megaphone held to his face, barking commands. Ignored. He drops the megaphone to his side, hangs his head, and collapses into a bench.

The yellow hats move in.

The smell of them makes me swoon—dried saliva and scalp, a sweet, fetid whiff of childhood. I think of Frank. Why is sanity so hard?

Watch the monkey scare the children. But they're not scared. I am. Watching them come at me. Cherry-cheeked. Swaths of black hair across foreheads. High ponytails like antennae. Tiny teeth crowded together, flashing like an animal's threat. There's silence for a moment as they encircle me. One boy, his chest heaving with excitement, pulls his arm back, raises one knee like a pitcher, and throws a handful of little pellets at me. Seeds. The rest of them follow suit, screaming and hitting one another as they wind up. They're chanting something rhythmical, like a nursery rhyme. The beans hit my map with a satisfying "Ping!" and

I stand there until the gentle patter ends, until the yelps and laughter and chanting fade into a honeyed gasping for breath.

The children are herded away by the teacher. Apologies are made. The yellow hats disappear into a cluster of cherry trees. I stand like a planet, the constellation of seeds radiating from me, spilling from my pockets. I see, as if for the first time, the quality of the air. Bluish light filtered through it. The sun, like a yolk hanging languorously behind the trees. The air with its giddy bite of anticipation. I breathe it in like anesthesia, but it doesn't put me to sleep. It wakes me up.

The day before I leave Canada, I go to see Frank at the group home. It's an ugly duplex on a street of ugly duplexes. A toothless middle-aged woman in a tube-top follows me from the street. "Can you buy me a coffee?" she whines.

"I'm in a hurry," I tell her.

The woman's expression barely passes to disappointed. A split second of the normal human condition. Then, like a skipping record, she asks me again, with the same hope and confidence, "Can you buy me a coffee?"

The past doesn't scar her.

I press a dollar into her palm. "Lucky bitch," I say.

Frank's room is neat. Books on the shelf. Towels on the racks. Cupboard doors shut. It scares me. Above his desk are two of his pen-and-ink drawings. One of Toronto City Hall. The other of a giant alien insect shooting a laser beam at a barn. Frank is sitting there at the desk. Just sitting there.

"Hey Frankie."

He turns and watches me. Then, finally, he says hello.

"I've come to say good-bye."

"Good-bye?"

"I'm going to Asia on Saturday. Don't know how long for."

"Acidophilus," he tells me.

"Thailand. India. Japan. What did you say?"

"To replace intestinal flora?"

"Oh. Like for Delhi Belly. Okay." *Acidophilus. Fuck.* "Frank are you doing okay?"

"I talk to someone every day."

"Like a doctor?" I ask.

He turns back to his desk. There's nothing on it. Not a pencil or a blotter.

"I have cable," he answers.

"Frank?" His face looks like a mask to me. "How do the drugs make you feel?" It's what I want to know.

"They don't make me feel," he tells me.

There's a parcel waiting for me at the guesthouse. A tiny box wrapped in paper and brown string. The sight of it startles me. No one knows where I am. I turn it in my hands. "Who left this?" I ask the girl. She leans in, stifles a giggle. "Handsome man. No hair. Five minutes before." I turn and run outside. Squint into the shadows. Suddenly the city is deserted. Just me and the cherry trees and their pink arms. My feet are bare. I grip the pavement with my toes. Rooted.

Frank with his wild mind. Dad with his shiny new family. Mom with her soft new lovers. And me. Me with the sweet pain of home.

The wind comes up. Cherry blossom petals rain down on me.

I tell myself, there is no happy ending. All the pieces do not fit together perfectly. Things are ragged and messy. We are torn apart by events. Put back together differently by others. And somehow everything is beautiful.

I undo the string. Take the top off the box and pull out a cloud of tissue. Nestled on a bed of satin is Kazu's finger. Unsullied by blood. A compass showing me the way. Out of the basin of Kyoto, off this beautiful island, back to the beginning. Home.

P.S.

Insights,
Interviews
& More . . .

Meet
Catherine Hanrahan

CATHERINE HANRAHAN was born in Montreal and raised in Halifax and Toronto. A self-described bookworm, early she vacillated between a desire to write and a desire to become a ballerina. "My parents gave me a typewriter and a copy of *How to Get Happily Published* for Christmas when I was ten," she says. "All literary ambitions were put on the back burner at age fourteen when I discovered boys."

Her father is a professor of finance, her mother a former laboratory instructor at the local university.

Young Catherine's reading interests ranged far and wide, from Frances Hodgson Burnett's *Secret Garden* to Graham Greene's *Dr. Fischer of Geneva, or The Bomb Party.* It was *The Secret Garden,* she says, which "more than

66 My parents gave me a typewriter and a copy of *How to Get Happily Published* for Christmas when I was ten. 99

anything made me want to become a writer." Graham Greene, on the other hand, became an influence courtesy of her mother, "a G.G. fanatic."

At college, Catherine first pursued an English degree, then moved on to comparative religion, and, finally, took a degree in philosophy. "I don't remember much—it's a bit hazy," she says. "But I was an aerobics instructor and I had rather scary biceps."

Over the years, she has worked a good many nonliterary jobs, including a host of waitress positions. Other jobs include bar hostess in Tokyo, English teacher, barmaid in London, and work at a New Age resort in Thailand ("I was barefoot for two months straight"). During periods of unemployment, she says, "I've made ends meet by filling out online surveys and selling off my shoe and handbag collection on eBay."

She is a past participant in the Wired Writing Studio at the Banff Centre for the Arts, to which she applied while living in Japan. "At the time," she recalls, "I had only written a few short stories and I didn't expect to get in, but I did, and the whole experience (two weeks residency and six months online mentorship) was incredibly encouraging. It really cemented my aspirations as a writer. After that I took writing as a career out of the ▶

Meet Catherine Hanrahan *(continued)*

pipe-dream slot and just went for it." What, then, does she think about writing workshops in general? "I'm not convinced that workshops make people write better," she says, "but they certainly provide structure and community. As an antidote to creative isolation, writing programs are brilliant."

The germ for *Lost Girls and Love Hotels* appeared in a short story published online at *Zoetrope All-Story Extra.* She submitted the story, "Watch the Monkey Scare the Children," through *Zoetrope*'s online workshop—which she calls her "link to the writing community"—while she was in Japan. Asked whether her story appealed to *Zoetrope* owing to a cinematic quality, she replies: "I'm not sure if it is cinematic so much as weird. Being a bit weird has always got me noticed."

Lost Girls and Love Hotels amassed approximately eight rejection slips, she says. How did she deal with the rejection? "Honestly, I've never been bothered by rejection. Doubt and the tendency towards despondency is something that all writers have to deal with. I deal with it by being very single-minded—I simply refuse to indulge myself in doubt. I'm reminded of that

66 Being a bit weird has always got me noticed. 99

Saturday Night Live skit where Stuart Smalley does the cheesy affirmations 'I'm good enough, I'm smart enough, and doggone it, people like me!' I did the writerly version of that. I got my fair share of rejections, but I just got on with it. I guess I'm stubborn. And maybe a bit of a born-again Pollyanna. And I have a fantastic agent (that helps, too).

Carol Shields once called Canada a "very good country for writers." "We don't," she explained, "have a long literary tradition. People aren't intimidated by the ghost of Hemingway or Faulkner." Catherine agrees. "Canada *is* a very good country for writers, but I would say it from a practical perspective. The Canadian government supports writers with grants. Canadians also read a lot—literary or nonmainstream books regularly top the bestseller list in Canada. I've spent much of my adult life as an expat, but it is always nice to come back home. For writers and artists there is definitely something nurturing about Canada."

Her parents remain highly supportive of her writing. "When the novel was accepted for publication, my parents asked me to send them a copy of the manuscript to read. I had to warn them about the sex and drugs in the story, ▶

" I had to warn my parents about the sex and drugs in the story, to which my dad responded, 'Well then send it in a plain brown wrapper.' "

Meet Catherine Hanrahan *(continued)*

to which my dad responded, 'Well then send it in a plain brown wrapper.' "

Catherine's weapon of choice is a Mac iBook. "I always write at cafés," she says. "I like the din of people around me. I also like coffee. Halfway through the novel I quit smoking, which was weird since in Japan there was always a cloud of ciggie smoke surrounding me when I wrote." Her beverage ritual looks something like this: coffee before 2 P.M., Guinness after.

Her hobbies are yoga and knitting. Asked about her enthusiasms, she quips, "Do high heels count as an enthusiasm?"

She is engaged to an English firefighter. "Andrew and I met in a bar in Vancouver," she says. "He was in Canada doing a Yoga teacher training course and I'd just finished doing a cleansing fast. When he overheard that I was breaking my fast with a pint of beer he knew we were meant for each other. We have barely been apart since then." ∾

> " When Andrew overheard that I was breaking my fast with a pint of beer he knew we were meant for each other. "

Writing a "Love Letter to Japan"

THE STORY BEHIND THE BOOK begins in Japan, where I lived for five years. It also begins with Hiroshi, the Japanese chef whom I dated on and off for three years. Like Kazu in the novel, Hiroshi was handsome, charismatic, and spoke a strangely poetic truncated English. Hiroshi is a book unto himself. During our relationship he was pressured by his family into an *omiae* (the polite Japanese term for an arranged marriage). He fell ill suddenly (just like in the soap operas). While hospitalized he was wheeled out of the institution in a tuxedo and married in a lavish ceremony (complete with a "fake" minister), all the while connected to an IV tube. He divorced soon after recovering from his illness, was briefly disowned by his parents, and after some struggles eventually realized his dream of opening his own restaurant.

Throughout our relationship Hiroshi and I would meet at love hotels. Sometimes we'd go to one down the street from my apartment, not because we had to hide away, but just for the fun of it.

As this drama unfolded I was

> 66 Throughout our relationship Hiroshi and I would meet at love hotels. Sometimes we'd go to one down the street from my apartment, not because we had to hide away, but just for the fun of it. 99

working for a big English conversation school company. Picture McDonald's, but instead of hamburgers, English conversation is hawked. Actually, the job wasn't all that bad. Better than my previous jobs in Japan, among them pronunciation corrector at a helicopter pilot school, hostess in a bar (lighting businessmen's cigarettes and brushing their hands off my knee), and a brief stint handing out packets of Kleenex in front of train stations.

The English conversation company also ran stewardess training courses. Being a flight attendant for a Japanese woman is equivalent to being a lawyer or physician in the West. Competition is fierce. Only women who graduate from prestigious universities have a shot at jobs with Japan Airlines or ANA. I felt this bizarre phenomenon begged to be explored in fiction. I had this idea about a very dislocated, depressed young woman who is plunked down in the world of the stewardess school. I'd been writing short stories for a year or so. One night in my tiny tatami mat room in Kyoto I wrote the first paragraph of a short story entitled "Watch the Monkey Scare the Children."

It took me a week to write the

story. I fell in love with the characters: Margaret, the world-weary English teacher fleeing from her past; and Frank, her sweetly weird brother who succumbs to the ravages of schizophrenia. The story was a success. It was picked up by an online edition of a literary magazine. I knew I'd hit on something and couldn't abandon Margaret and Frank. I decided to turn the story into a novel.

But the story needed something else when expanded to novel length. It needed romance. I created Kazu, a character whose life bears only a faint resemblance to Hiroshi's, but who embodies all of his sexy foreign appeal, his essential goodness, and his penchant for love hotel trysts.

The novel took two years to finish, and during that time I decided to leave Japan and return to Canada. In a strange way it was easier to write about Japan when I was thousands of miles away, as though time and distance called into relief all that is bizarre and beautiful about living in Tokyo. In a way, the novel is my love letter to Japan, the country that I grew to admire and respect fiercely, and to Hiroshi, who was a foreign country unto himself. ❧

> **❝** The novel took two years to finish, and during that time I decided to leave Japan. In a strange way it was easier to write about Japan when I was thousands of miles away. **❞**

"Miss Foreigner! Go back. It's sleeping time."
Catherine Hanrahan on Japan's Love Hotels

WHILE LIVING IN JAPAN I came up with the idea of a novel set in love hotels, the kitschy, pay-by-the-hour inns huddled around train stations and nightspots. The *rabu-hoteru,* I thought, would be the perfect setting for my story of culture shock, sex, and death in turn-of-the-millennium Tokyo. So, with the kind assistance of my Japanese boyfriend I set out to do *research*. What I found was a peculiarly Japanese institution that illuminates a guilt-free, playful attitude toward sex and a love of all things cheesy.

To those who travel to Japan in search of Zen gardens and geisha the idea of visiting gaudy two-hour love nests with revolving beds might seem ludicrous. In many ways, though, going to a love hotel is the quintessential Japanese experience. It's practical, almost completely automated, flashy, gaudy, and surprisingly cheap.

In Japan's predominantly urban society, where more often than not three generations of a family live together in small apartments, love

66 To those who travel to Japan in search of Zen gardens and geisha the idea of visiting gaudy two-hour love nests with revolving beds might seem ludicrous. 99

hotels provide a much-needed private place for sex. Parents with small children use love hotels; so do grandparents. Pretty much everyone seems to use them. It's all very matter-of-fact: no moral issues, no "not in my neighborhood." If anything, love hotels are becoming *more* acceptable in Japanese society. The *rabu-hoteru* is going upscale. Most young people no longer use the term "love hotel," but prefer the classier "fashion hotel" moniker.

Some trace the origin of the modern love hotel to small pensions that were set up next to shrines and temples for pilgrims to "relax" after a tough day of meditating. This juxtaposition of the sacred and profane makes sense if you look at the Japanese *kami* or gods, who like those of Greek legend were quite the randy bunch.

Love hotels began to flourish in the 1950s, when the typical "sex and shower" establishment began to pop up near train stations in big cities. At first these hotels aped the *ryokan*, or traditional Japanese inn, with simple tatami mat floors and shoji screen partitions. But come the 1960s hotels catering to the "Western" idea of romance started to appear. The Japanese may have no word for kitsch, but it is alive and well at the love hotel. With ▶

"Miss Foreigner! Go back. It's sleeping time." *(continued)*

their plastic tile and fake wood, their Corinthian columns and rococo bathrooms, the modern love hotel is so bad it's good.

Most love hotels operate on similar systems. To ensure their guests can fully relax love hotels are models of discretion. Anonymity is assured through the apparent absence of human staff. Underground parking and entrances to the hotels are hidden from view. Guests are greeted in the lobby with a backlit panel displaying photographs of available rooms. Most love hotels offer rooms for a "rest" (usually one to three hours and ranging in price from thirty to fifty dollars) and a stay (usually ten P.M. to noon the next day for sixty to one hundred dollars). Lights on the floor act as a sparkly trail to the love nest, which is unlocked and waiting.

Foreigners visiting love hotels are often baffled by some of the establishments' protocol. The doors to the rooms, for example, cannot be opened from inside in most hotels. Locks are encased in a plastic dome and the rooms can only be exited by calling reception and asking the attendant to remotely unlock the door. A friend of

66 To ensure their guests can fully relax love hotels are models of discretion. 99

mine found herself trapped in a love hotel room, unable to read the sign on the door and unable to communicate in Japanese with the reception desk. She and her boyfriend ended up pounding on the wall until a horrified attendant arrived at the door and clicked his tongue at them for five minutes. I've always thought that this system made for very effective fire traps, but my Japanese friends insist that it is necessary. If you could simply open the door and stroll into the hallways at will, two couples could bump into one another and lose face.

Then there's the issue of how to pay. Old-school love hotels still use the vacuum chute system. I like this one best. You call the front desk and ask for your bill and *swoosh!*—a plastic tube appears in a vacuum chute embedded in the wall. You put your cash in the tube (Japan is predominantly a cash-only society), push a button, and *swoosh!*— the money disappears into the chute, discretion assured. In other hotels you pay on your way out. A disembodied pair of hands behind a small curtained window near the door takes your money and you're on your way.

Inside, the rooms range from ▶

" Then there's the issue of how to pay. Old-school love hotels still use the vacuum chute system. I like this one best. "

"Miss Foreigner! Go back. It's sleeping time." *(continued)*

standard hotel fare to Disneyesque castle interiors to S&M dungeons, and are fully automated. The TV, radio, and lights can be controlled from the headboard. Drinks, snacks, and sex toys (usually displayed on a "Sexy Goods" menu) can be bought from in-room vending machines or from room service. Most rooms offer an astounding array of mood music choices, ranging from Japanese pop to Swiss yodeling. There's usually an alibi station as well— the sounds of traffic or the pitch and roll of a train—just in case one's significant other calls.

In recent years, partly due to the introduction by the Japanese government of the "New Public Morals Act," love hotels have cleaned up their sleazy image. Catering more and more to the "OL" market (office ladies, or young unmarried working women), the porn is making room for DVD libraries featuring *Breakfast at Tiffany's.* Romantic themes are replacing the male-oriented race car and spaceship rooms. Women can buy cutesy "fashion hotel" guidebooks which detail the perfect hotel in which to "rest" after a romantic date.

My favorite love hotels were those

with outrageously tacky theme rooms—revolving merry-go-round beds, spaceship showers—but my boyfriend, apparently like most hip young Japanese, preferred the "classy" establishments. These hotels, which seemed to me to be a bad satire of Western "luxury," attract the martini-sipping clubgoers with their panoramic views, luxury toiletries, and faux French provincial furniture.

The continuing recession has inspired some innovative marketing practices. One hotel offered a free trip to Tokyo Disneyland for any couple who used each of its twenty-four rooms in a six-month period. A sex marathon for Mickey Mouse—what could be more Japanese? One establishment we visited rewarded us for our patronage with two ballpoint pens and a comb. At another hotel our receipt was accompanied by coupons for free soft-serve ice-cream cones.

In all the love hotels I visited I only encountered a staff member once. It was in a simple hotel near Narita airport in Tokyo. I was staying there overnight to avoid an early morning trip to catch my flight. In the middle of the night I ventured out into the hall, having run ▶

66 My favorite love hotels were those with outrageously tacky theme rooms—revolving merry-go-round beds, spaceship showers. 99

"Miss Foreigner! Go back. It's sleeping time." *(continued)*

out of bottled water in the stuffy room (at this particular hotel I wasn't locked in). I wandered around for a bit, feeling a little naughty and curious, until a door disguised as part of the wall in the lobby opened. A tiny old man in a tight-fitting blue suit hobbled out and in a stage whisper called to me, "Miss Foreigner! Go back. It's sleeping time." ∽

Don't miss the next book by your favorite author. Sign up now for AuthorTracker by visiting www.AuthorTracker.com.